He thought of his own flesh decomposing.

The whole fleshly universe decomposing.

It would be over in an instant,

    the way the universe measures time.

A wild pulse lost in some breeze.

Time was running out when McKie found the last Caleban; damaged, fading, nearly incoherent—or was she? He was pathetically unable to communicate with the tormented creature—much less free her from the ruthless force of evil which had enslaved her awesome power...and which relentlessly sought the annihilation of sentient life.

Berkley Books by Frank Herbert

WHIPPING STAR
Frank Herbert

BERKLEY BOOKS, NEW YORK

*To Lurton Blassingame, who helped buy the time for
this book, dedicated with affection and admiration*

A shorter version of this book appeared in *Worlds of If Science
Fiction* for December 1969 — March 1970. Copyright © 1969,
1970 by Galaxy Publishing Corporation.

WHIPPING STAR

A Berkley Book / published by arrangement with
the author

PRINTING HISTORY
Berkley Medallion edition / September 1977
Seventeenth printing / September 1983
Eighteenth printing / April 1984

ISBN: 0-425-06997-4

A BERKLEY BOOK ® TM 757,375
The name "BERKLEY" and the stylized "B" with design
are trademarks belonging to Berkley Publishing Corporation.
PRINTED IN THE UNITED STATES OF AMERICA

A BuSab agent must begin by learning the linquis-tic modes and action limits (usually self-imposed) of the societies he treats. The agent seeks data on the functional relationships which derive from our com-mon universe and which arise from interdependen-cies. Such interdependencies are the frequent first victims of word-illusions. Societies based on igno-rance of original interdependencies come sooner or later to stalemate. Too long frozen, such societies die.

—BuSab Manual

Furuneo was his name. Alichino Furuneo. He reminded himself of this as he rode into the city to make the long-distance call. It was wise to firm up the ego before such a call. He was sixty-seven years old and could remember many cases where people had lost their identity in the sniggertrance of communication between star systems. More than the cost and the mind-crawling sensation of dealing with a Taprisiot transmitter, this uncertainty factor tended to keep down the number of calls. But Furuneo didn't feel he could trust anyone else with this call to Jorj X. McKie, Saboteur Extraordinary.

It was 8:08 A.M. local at Furuneo's position on the planet called Cordiality of the Sfich system.

"This is going to be very difficult, I suspect," he mut-tered, speaking at (but not to) the two enforcers he had brought along to guard his privacy.

They didn't even nod, realizing no reply was expected.

It was still cool from the night wind which blew across the snow plains of the Billy Mountains down to the sea. They had driven here into Division City from Furuneo's mountain fortress, riding in an ordinary groundcar, not attempting to hide or disguise their association with the Bureau of Sabo-

1

tage, but not seeking to attract attention, either. Many sentients had reason to resent the Bureau.

Furuneo had ordered the car left outside the city's Pedestrian Central, and they had come the rest of the way on foot like ordinary citizens.

Ten minutes ago they had entered the reception room of this building. It was a Taprisiot breeding center, one of only about twenty known to exist in the universe, quite an honor for a minor planet like Cordiality.

The reception room was no more than fifteen meters wide, perhaps thirty-five long. It had tan walls with pitted marks in them as though they had been soft once and someone had thrown a small ball at them according to some random whim. Along the right side across from where Furuneo stood with his enforcers was a high bench. It occupied three-fourths of the long wall. Multi-faceted rotating lights above it cast patterned shadows onto the face of the bench and the Taprisiot standing atop it.

Taprisiots came in odd shapes like sawed-off lengths of burned conifers, with stub limbs jutting every which way, needlelike speech appendages fluttering even when they remained silent. This one's skidfeet beat a nervous rhythm on the surface where it stood.

For the third time since entering, Furuneo asked, "Are you the transmitter?"

No answer.

Taprisiots were like that. No sense getting angry. It did no good. Furuneo allowed himself to be annoyed, though. Damned Taprisiots!

One of the enforcers behind Furuneo cleared his throat.

Damn this delay! Furuneo thought.

The whole Bureau had been in a state of jitters ever since the max-alert message on the Abnethe case. This call he was preparing to make might be their first real break. He sensed the fragile urgency of it. It could be the most important call he had ever made. And directly to McKie, at that.

The sun, barely over the Billy Mountains, spread an orange fan of light around him from the windowed doorway through which they had entered.

"Looks like it's gonna be a long wait for this Tappy," one of his enforcers muttered.

Furuneo nodded curtly. He had learned several degrees of patience in sixty-seven years, especially on his way up the ladder to his present position as planetary agent for the Bureau. There was only one thing to do here: wait it out quietly. Taprisiots took their own time for whatever mysterious reasons. There was no other *store,* though, where he could buy the service he needed now. Without a Taprisiot transmitter, you didn't make real-time calls across interstellar space.

Strange, this Taprsiot talent—used by so many sentients without understanding. The sensational press abounded with theories on how it was accomplished. For all anyone knew, one of the theories could be right. Perhaps Taprisiots *did* make these calls in a way akin to the data linkage among Pan Spechi crèche mates—not that this was understood, either.

It was Furuneo's belief that Taprisiots distorted space in a way similar to that of a Caleban jumpdoor, sliding between the dimensions. If that was really what Caleban jumpdoors did. Most experts denied this theory, pointing out that it would require energies equivalent to those produced by fair-sized stars.

Whatever Taprisiots did to make a call, one thing was certain: It involved the human pineal gland or its equivalent among other sentients.

The Taprisiot on the high bench began moving from side to side.

"Maybe we're getting through to it," Furuneo said.

He composed his features, suppressed his feelings of unease. This was, after all, a Taprisiot breeding center. Xenobiologists said Taprisiot reproduction was all quite tame, but Xenos didn't know everything. Look at the mess they'd made of analyzing the PanSpechi Con-Sentiency.

"Putcha, putcha, putcha," the Taprisiot on the bench said, squeaking its speech needles.

"Something wrong?" one of the enforcers asked.

"How the devil do I know?" Furuneo snapped. He faced the Taprisiot, said, "Are you the transmitter?"

"Putcha, putcha, putcha," the Taprisiot said. "This is a remark which I will now translate in the only way that may make sense to ones like yourselves of Sol/Earth ancestry. What I said was, 'I question your sincerity.' "

"You gotta justify your sincerity to a damn Taprisiot?" one of the enforcers asked. "Seems to me . . ."

"Nobody asked you!" Furuneo cut him off. Any probing attack by a Taprisiot was likely a greeting. Didn't the fool know this?

Furuneo separated himself from the enforcers, crossed to a position below the bench. "I wish to make a call to Saboteur Extraordinary Jorj X. McKie," he said. "Your robogreeter recognized and idenitifed me and took my creditchit. Are you the transmitter?"

"Where is this Jorj X. McKie?" the Taprisiot asked.

"If I knew, I'd be off to him in person through a jumpdoor," Furuneo said. "This is an important call. Are you the transmitter?"

"Date, time, and place," the Taprisiot said.

Furuneo sighed and relaxed. He glanced back at the enforcers, motioned them to take up stations at the room's two doors, waited while they obeyed. Wouldn't do to have this call overheard. He turned then, gave the required local coordinates.

"You will sit on floor," the Taprisiot said.

"Thank the immortals for that," Furuneo muttered. He'd once made a call where the transmitter had led him to a mountainside in wind and driving rain and made him stretch out, head lower than feet, before opening the overspace contact. It had had something to do with "refining the embedment," whatever that meant. He'd reported the incident to the Bureau's data center, where they hoped one day to solve the Taprisiot secret, but the call had cost him several weeks with an upper respiratory infection.

Furuneo sat.

Damn! The floor was cold!

Furuneo was a tall man, two meters in bare feet, eighty-four standard kilos. His hair was black with a dusting of grey at the ears. He had a thick nose and wide mouth with an oddly straight lower lip. He favored his left hip as he sat. A disgruntled citizen had broken it during one of his early tours with the Bureau. The injury defied all the medics who had told him, "It won't bother you a bit after it's healed."

"Close eyes," the Taprisiot squeaked.

4

Furuneo obeyed, tried to squirm into a more comfortable position on the cold, hard floor, gave it up.

"Think of contact," the Taprisiot ordered.

Furuneo thought of Jorj X. McKie, building the image in his mind—squat little man, angry red hair, face like a disgruntled frog.

Contact began with tendrils of cloying awareness. Furuneo became in his own mind a red flow sung to the tune of a silver lyre. His body went remote. Awareness rotated above a strange landscape. The sky was an infinite circle with its horizon slowly turning. He sensed the stars engulfed in loneliness.

"What the ten million devils!"

The thought exploded across Furuneo. There was no evading it. He recognized it at once. Contactees frequently resented the call. They couldn't reject it, no matter what they were doing at the time, but they could make the caller feel their displeasure.

"It never fails! It never fails!"

McKie would be jerked to full inner awareness now, his pineal gland ignited by the long-distance contact.

Furuneo settled himself to wait out the curses. When they had subsided sufficiently, he identified himself, said, "I regret any inconvenience I may have caused, but the max-alert failed to say where you could be located. You must know I would not have called unless it were important."

A more or less standard opening.

"How the hell do I know whether your call's important?" McKie demanded. "Stop babbling and get on with it!"

This was an unusual extension of anger even for the volatile McKie. "Did I interrupt something important?" Furuneo ventured.

"I was just standing here in a telicourt getting a divorce!" McKie said. "Can't you imagine what a great time everyone here's having, watching me mubble-dubble to myself in a sniggertrance? Get to the business!"

"A Caleban Beachball washed ashore last night below Division City here on Cordiality," Furuneo said. "In view of all the deaths and insanity and the max-alert message from

5

the Bureau, I thought I'd better call you at once. It's still your case, isn't it?''

"Is this your idea of a joke?" McKie demanded.

In lieu of red tape, Furuneo cautioned himself, thinking of the Bureau maxim. It was a private thought, but McKie no doubt was catching the mood of it.

"Well?" McKie demanded.

Was McKie deliberately trying to unnerve him? Furuneo wondered. How could the Bureau's prime function—to slow the processes of government—remain operative on an internal matter such as this call? Agents were duty bound to encourage anger in government because it exposed the unstable, temperamental types, the ones who lacked the necessary personal control and ability to think under psychic stress, but why carry this duty over to a call from a fellow agent?

Some of these thoughts obviously bled through the Taprisiot transmitter because McKie reflected them, enveloping Furuneo in a mental sneer.

"You lotsa time unthink yourself," McKie said.

Furuneo shuddered, recovered his sense of self. Ahhh, that had been close. He'd almost lost his ego! Only the veiled warning in McKie's words had alerted him, allowing recovery. Furuneo began casting about in his mind for another interpretation of McKie's reaction. Interrupting the divorce could not account for it. If the stories were true, the ugly little agent had been married fifty or more times.

"Are you still interested in the Beachball?" Furuneo ventured.

"Is there a Caleban in it?"

"Presumably."

"You haven't investigated?" McKie's mental tone said Furuneo had been entrusted with a most crucial operation and had failed because of inherent stupidity.

Now fully alert to some unspoken danger, Furuneo said, "I acted as my orders instructed."

"Orders!" McKee sneered.

"I'm supposed to be angry, eh?" Furuneo asked.

"I'll be there as fast as I can get service—within eight standard hours at the most," McKie said. "Your *orders,* meanwhile, are to keep that Beachball under constant observation. The observers must be hopped up on *angeret*. It's their only protection.''

''Constant observation,'' Furuneo said.

''If a Caleban emerges, you're to detain it by any means possible.''

''A Caleban . . . detain it?''

''Engage it in conversation, request its cooperation, anything,'' McKie said. His mental emphasis added that it was odd a Bureau agent should have to ask about throwing a monkey wrench into someone's activities.

''Eight hours,'' Furuneo said.

''And don't forget the angeret.''

A Bureau is a life form and the Bureaucrat one of its cells. This analogy teaches us which are the more important cells, which in greatest peril, which most easily replaced, and how easy it is to be mediocre.

—Later Writings of Bildoon IV

McKie, on the honeymoon planet of Tutalsee, took an hour to complete his divorce, then returned to the float-home they had moored beside an island of love flowers. Even the nepenthe of Tutalsee had failed him, McKie thought. This marriage had been wasted effort. His ex hadn't known enough about Mliss Abnethe despite their reported former association. But that had been on another world.

This wife had been his fifty-fourth, somewhat lighter of skin than any of the others and more than a bit of a shrew. It had not been her first marriage, and she had shown early suspicions of McKie's secondary motives.

Reflection made McKie feel guilty. He put such feelings aside savagely. There was no time for nicety. Too much was at stake. Stupid female!

She had already vacated the float-home, and McKie could sense the living entity's resentment. He had shattered the idyll which the float-home had been conditioned to create. The float-home would return to its former affability once he was gone. They were gentle creatures, susceptible to sentient irritation.

McKie packed, leaving his toolkit aside. He examined it: a selection of stims, plastipicks, explosives in various denominations, raygens, multigoggles, pentrates, a wad of uniflesh, solvos, miniputer, Taprisiot life monitor, holoscan blanks, rupters, comparators . . . all in order. The toolkit was a fitted wallet which he concealed in an inner pocket of his nondescript jacket.

He packed a few changes of clothing in a single bag,

consigned the rest of his possessions to BuSab storage, left them for pickup in a sealpack which he stored on a couple of chairdogs. They appeared to share the float-home's resentment. They remained immobile even when he patted them affectionately.

Ah, well. . . .

He still felt guilty.

McKie sighed, took out his S'eye key. This jump was going to cost the Bureau megacredits. Cordiality lay halfway across their universe.

Jumpdoors still seemed to be working, but it disturbed McKie that he must make this journey by a means which was dependent upon a Caleban. Eerie situation. S'eye jumpdoors had become so common that most sentients accepted them without question. McKie had shared this common acceptance before the max-alert. Now he wondered at himself. Casual acceptance demonstrated how easily rational thought could be directed by wishful thinking. This was a common susceptibility of all sentients. The Caleban jumpdoor had been fully accepted by the Confederated Sentients for some ninety standard years. But in that time, only eighty-three Calebans were known to have identified themselves.

McKie flipped the key in his hand, caught it deftly.

Why had the Calebans refused to part with their gift unless everyone agreed to call it a "S'eye"? What was so important about a name?

I should be on my way, McKie told himself. Still he delayed.

Eighty-three Calebans.

The max-alert had been explicit in its demand for secrecy and its outline of the problem: Calebans had been disappearing one by one. Disappearing—if that was what the Caleban manifestation could be called. And each *disappearance* had been accompanied by a massive wave of sentient deaths and insanity.

No question why the problem had been dumped in BuSab's lap instead of onto some police agency. Government fought back wherever it could: Powerful men hoped to discredit BuSab. McKie found his own share of disturbance in wondering about the hidden possibilities in the selection of himself as the sentient to tackle this.

9

Who hates me? he wondered as he used his personally tuned key in the jumpdoor. The answer was that many people hated him. Millions of people.

The jumpdoor began to hum with its aura of terrifying energies. The door's vortal tube snapped open. McKie tensed himself for the syrupy resistance to jumpdoor passage, stepped through the tube. It was like swimming in air become molasses—perfectly normal-appearing air. But molasses.

McKie found himself in a rather ordinary office: the usual humdrum whirldesk, alert-flicker light patterns cascading from the ceiling, a view out one transparent wall onto a mountainside. In the distance the rooftops of Division City lay beneath dull gray clouds, with a luminous silver sea beyond. McKie's implated brainclock told him it was late afternoon, the eighteenth hour of a twenty-six-hour day. This was Cordiality, a world 200,000 light-years from Tutalsee's planetary ocean.

Behind him, the jumpdoor's vortal tube snapped closed with a crackling sound like the discharge of electricity. A faint ozone smell permeated the air.

The room's standard-model chairdogs had been well trained to comfort their masters, McKie noted. One of them nudged him behind the knees until he dropped his bag and took a reluctant seat. The chairdog began massaging his back. Obviously it had been instructed to make him comfortable while someone was summoned.

McKie tuned himself to the faint sounds of normality around him. Footsteps of a sentient could be heard in an outer passage. A Wreave by the sound of it: that peculiar dragging of the heel on a favored foot. There was a dim conversation somewhere, and McKie could make out a few Lingua-galach words, but it sounded like a multilingual conversation.

He began fidgeting, which set the chairdog into a burst of rippling movements to soothe him. Enforced idleness nagged at him. Where was Furuneo? McKie chided himself. Furuneo probably had many planetary duties as BuSab agent here. And he couldn't know the full urgency of their problem. This might be one of the planets where BuSab was spread thin. The gods of immortality knew the Bureau could always find work.

McKie began reflecting on his role in the affairs of sentiency. Once, long centuries past, con-sentients with a psychological compulsion to "do good" had captured the government. Unaware of the writhing complexities, the mingled guilts and self-punishments, beneath their compulsion, they had eliminated virtually all delays and red tape from government. The great machine with its blundering power over sentient life had slipped into high gear, had moved faster and faster. Laws had been conceived and passed in the same hour. Appropriations had flashed into being and were spent in a fortnight. New bureaus for the most improbable purposes had leaped into existence and proliferated like some insane fungus.

Government had become a great destructive wheel without a governor, whirling with such frantic speed that it spread chaos wherever it touched.

In desperation, a handful of sentients had conceived the Sabotage Corps to slow that wheel. There had been bloodshed and other degrees of violence, but the wheel had been slowed. In time, the Corps had become a Bureau, and the Bureau was whatever it was today—an organization headed into its own corridors of entropy, a group of sentients who preferred subtle diversion to violence . . . but were prepared for violence when the need arose.

A door slid back on McKie's right. His chairdog became still. Furuneo entered, brushing a hand through the band of grey hair at his left ear. His wide mouth was held in a straight line, a suggestion of sourness about it.

"You're early," he said, patting a chairdog into place across from McKie and seating himself.

"Is this place safe?" McKie asked. He glanced at the wall where the S'eye had disgorged him. The jumpdoor was gone.

"I've moved the door back downstairs through its own tube," Furuneo said. "This place is as private as I can make it." He sat back, waiting for McKie to explain.

"That Beachball still down there?" McKie nodded toward the transparent wall and the distant sea.

"My men have orders to call me if it makes any move," Furuneo said. "It was washed ashore just like I said, embedded itself in a rock outcropping, and hasn't moved since."

11

"Embedded itself?"

"That's how it seems."

"No sign of anything in it?"

"Not that we can see. The Ball does appear to be a bit . . . banged up. There are some pitting and a few external scars. What's this all about?"

"No doubt you've heard of Mliss Abnethe?"

"Who hasn't?"

"She recently spent some of her quintillions to hire a Caleban."

"Hire a . . ." Furuneo shook his head. "I didn't know it could be done."

"Neither did anyone else."

"I read the max-alert," Furuneo said. "Abnethe's connection with the case wasn't explained."

"She's a bit kinky about floggings, you know," McKie said.

"I thought she was treated for that."

"Yeah, but it didn't eliminate the root of her problem. It just fixed her so she couldn't stand the sight of a sentient suffering."

"So?"

"Her solution, naturally, was to hire a Caleban."

"As a victim!" Furuneo said.

Furuneo was beginning to understand, McKie saw. Someone had once said the problem with Calebans was that they presented no patterns you could recognize. This was true, of course. If you could imagine an *actuality,* a being whose presence could not be denied but who left your senses dangling every time you tried to look at it—then you could imagine a Caleban.

"They're shuttered windows opening onto eternity," as the poet Masarard put it.

In the first Caleban days, McKie had attended every Bureau lecture and briefing about them. He tried to recall one of those sessions now, prompted by a nagging sensation that it had contained something of value to his present problem. It had been something about "communications difficulties within an aura of affliction." The precise content eluded him. Odd, he thought. It was as though the Calebans' crumbled projection created an effect on sentient memory akin to their effect on sentient vision.

Here lay the true source of sentient uneasiness about Calebans. Their artifacts were real—the S'eye jumpdoors, the Beachballs in which they were reputed to live—but no one had ever really *seen* a Caleban.

Furuneo, watching the fat little gnome of an agent sit there thinking, recalled the snide story about McKie, that he had been in BuSab since the day before he was born.

"She's hired a whipping boy, eh?" Furuneo asked.

"That's about it."

"The max-alert spoke of deaths, insanity. . . ."

"Are all your people dosed with *angeret?*" McKie asked.

"I got the message, McKie."

"Good. Anger seems to afford some protection."

"What exactly is going on?"

"Calebans have been . . . vanishing," McKie said. "Every time one of them goes, there are quite a few deaths and . . . other unpleasant effects—physical and mental crippling, insanity. . . ."

Furuneo nodded in the direction of the sea, leaving his question unspoken.

McKie shrugged. "We'll have to go take a look. The hell of it is, up until your call there seemed to be only one Caleban left in the universe, the one Abnethe hired."

"How're you going to handle this?"

"That's a beautiful question," McKie said.

"Abnethe's Caleban," Furuneo said. "It have anything to say by way of explanation?"

"Haven't been able to interview it," McKie said. "We don't know where she's hidden herself—or it."

"Don't know. . . ." Furuneo blinked. "Cordiality's pretty much of a backwater."

"That's what I've been thinking. You said this Beachball was a little the worse for wear?"

"That's odd, isn't it?"

"Another oddity among many."

"They say a Caleban doesn't get very far from its Ball," Furuneo said. "And they like to park 'em near water."

13

"How much of an attempt did you make to communicate with it?"

"The usual. How'd you find out about Abnethe hiring a Caleban?"

"She bragged to a friend who bragged to a friend who- . . . . And one of the other Calebans dropped a hint before disappearing."

"Any doubt the disappearances and the rest of it are tied together?"

"Let's go knock on this thing's door and find out," McKie said.

Language is a kind of code dependent upon the life rhythms of the species which originated the language. Unless you learn those rhythms, the code remains mostly unintelligible.

—BuSab Manual

McKie's immediate ex-wife had adopted an early attitude of resentment toward BuSab. "They use you!" she had protested.

He had thought about that for a few minutes, wondering if it might be the reason he found it so easy to use others. She was right, of course.

McKie thought about her words now as he and Furuneo sped by groundcar toward the Cordiality coast. The question in McKie's mind was, How are they using me this time? Setting aside the possibility that he had been offered up as a sacrifice, there were still many possibilities in reserve. Was it his legal training they needed? Or had they been prompted by his unorthodox approach to interspecies relationships? Obviously they entertained some hope for a special sort of official sabotage—but what sort? Why had his instructions been so incomplete?

"You will seek out and contact the Caleban which has been hired by Madame Mliss Abnethe, or find any other Caleban available for sentient contact, and you will take appropriate action."

Appropriate action?

McKie shook his head.

"Why'd they choose you for this gig?" Furuneo asked.

"They know how to use me," McKie said.

The groundcar, driven by an enforcer, negotiated a sharp turn, and a vista of rocky shore opened before them. Something glittered in the distance among black lava palisades, and McKie noted two aircraft hovering above the rocks.

"That it?" he asked.

"Yes."

"What's the local time?"

"About two and a half hours to sunset," Furuneo said, correctly interpreting McKie's concern. "Will the *angeret* protect us if there's a Caleban in that thing and it decides to . . . disappear?"

"I sincerely hope so," McKie said. "Why didn't you bring us by aircar?"

"People here on Cordiality are used to seeing me in a groundcar unless I'm on official business and require speed."

"You mean nobody knows about this thing yet?"

"Just the coastwatchers for this stretch, and they're on my payroll."

"You run a pretty tight operation here," McKie said. "Aren't you afraid of getting too efficient?"

"I do my best," Furuneo said. He tapped the driver's shoulder.

The groundcar pulled to a stop at a turnaround which looked down onto a reach of rocky islands and a low lava shelf where the Caleban Beachball had come to rest. "You know, I keep wondering if we really know what those Beachballs are."

"They're homes," McKie grunted.

"So everybody says."

Furuneo got out. A cold wind set his hip aching. "We walk from here," he said.

There were times during the climb down the narrow path to the lava shelf when McKie felt thankful he had been fitted with a gravity web beneath his skin. If he fell, it would limit his rate of descent to a non-injurious speed. But there was nothing it could do about any beating he might receive in the surf at the base of the palisades, and if offered no protection at all against the chill wind and the driving spray.

He wished he'd worn a heatsuit.

"It's colder than I expected," Furuneo said, limping out onto the lava shelf. He waved to the aircars. One dipped its wings, maintaining its place in a slow, circling track above the Beachball.

16

Furuneo struck out across the shelf and McKie followed, jumped across a tidal pool, blinked and bent his head against a gust of windborne spray. The pounding of the surf on the rocks was loud here. They had to raise their voices to make themselves understood.

"You see?" Furuneo shouted. "Looks like it's been banged around a bit."

"Those things are supposed to be indestructible," McKie said.

The Beachball was some six meters in diameter. It sat solidly on the shelf, about half a meter of its bottom surface hidden by a depression in the rock, as though it had melted out a resting place.

McKie led the way up to the lee of the Ball, passing Furuneo in the last few meters. He stood there, hands in pockets, shivering. The round surface of the Ball failed to cut off the cold wind.

"It's bigger than I expected," he said as Furuneo stopped beside him.

"First one you've ever seen close up?"

"Yeah."

McKie passed his gaze across the thing. Knobs and indentations marked the opaque metallic surface. It seemed to him the surface variations carried some pattern. Sensors, perhaps? Controls of some kind? Directly in front of him there was what appeared to be a crackled mark, perhaps from a collision. It lay just below the surface, presenting no roughness to McKie's exploring hand.

"What if they're wrong about these things?" Furuneo asked.

"Mmmm?"

"What if they aren't Caleban homes?"

"Don't know. Do you recall the drill?"

"You find a 'nippled extrusion' and you knock on it. We tried that. There's one just around to your left."

McKie worked his way around in that direction, getting drenched by a wind-driven spray in the process. He reached up, still shivering from the cold, knocked at the indicated extrusion.

Nothing happened.

"Every briefing I ever attended says there's a door in these things somewhere," McKie grumbled.

"But they don't say the door opens every time you knock," Furuneo said.

McKie continued working his way around the Ball, found another nippled extrusion, knocked.

Nothing.

"We tried that one, too," Furuneo said.

"I feel like a damn fool," McKie said.

"Maybe there's nobody home."

"Remote control?" McKie asked.

"Or abandoned—a derelict."

McKie pointed to a thin green line about a meter long on the Ball's windward surface. "What's that?"

Furuneo hunched his shoulders against spray and wind, stared at the line. "Don't recall seeing it."

"I wish we knew a lot more about these damn things," McKie grumbled.

"Maybe we aren't knocking loud enough," Furuneo said.

McKie pursed his lips in thought. Presently he took out his toolkit, extracted a lump of low-grade explosive. "Go back on the other side," he said.

"You sure you ought to try that?" Furuneo asked.

"No."

"Well—" Furuneo shrugged, retreated around the Ball.

McKie applied a strip of the explosive along the green line, attached a time-thread, joined Furuneo.

Presently, there came a dull thump that was almost drowned by the surf.

McKie felt an abrupt inner silence, found himself wondering, *What if the Caleban gets angry and springs a weapon we've never heard of?* He darted around to the windward side.

An oval hole had appeared above the green line as though a plug had been sucked into the Ball.

"Guess you pushed the right button," Furuneo said.

McKie suppressed a feeling of irritation which he knew to be mostly *angeret* effect, said, "Yeah. Give me a leg up." Furuneo, he noted, was controlling the drug reaction almost perfectly.

18

With Furuneo's help McKie clambered into the open port, stared inside. Dull purple light greeted him, a suggestion of movement within the dimness.

"See anything?" Furuneo called.

"Don't know." McKie scrambled inside, dropped to a carpeted floor. He crouched, studied his surroundings in the purple glow. His teeth clattered from the cold. The room around him apparently occupied the entire center of the Ball—low ceiling, flickering rainbows against the inner surface on his left, a giant soup-spoon shape jutting into the room directly across from him, tiny spools, handles, and knobs against the wall on his right.

The sense of movement originated in the spoon bowl.

Abruptly, McKie realized he was in the presence of a Caleban.

"What do you see?" Furuneo called.

Without taking his gaze from the spoon, McKie turned his head slightly. "There's a Caleban in here."

"Shall I come in?"

"No. Tell your men and sit tight."

"Right."

McKie returned his full attention to the bowl of the spoon. His throat felt dry. He'd never before been alone in the presence of a Caleban. This was a position usually reserved for scientific investigators armed with esoteric instruments.

"I'm . . . ah, Jorj X. McKie, Bureau of Sabotage," he said.

There was a stirring at the spoon, an effect of radiated meaning immediately behind the movement: "I make your acquaintance."

McKie found himself recalling Masarard's poetic description in *Conversation With a Caleban.*

"Who can say how a Caleban speaks?" Masarard had written. *"Their words come at you like the corruscating of a nine-ribbon Sojeu barber pole. The insensitive way such words radiate. I say the Caleban speaks. When words are sent, is that not speech? Send me your words, Caleban, and I will tell the universe of your wisdom."*

Having experienced the Caleban's words, McKie decided Masarard was a pretentious ass. The Caleban radiated. Its

19

communication registered in the sentient mind as sound, but the ears denied they had heard anything. It was the same order of effect that Calebans had on the eyes. You felt you were seeing something, but the visual centers refused to agree.

"I hope my . . . ah, I didn't disturb you," McKie said.

"I possess no referent for disturb," the Caleban said. "You bring a companion?"

"My companion's outside," McKie said. *No referent for disturb?*

"Invite your companion," the Caleban said.

McKie hesitated, then, "Furuneo! C'mon in."

The planetary agent joined him, crouched at McKie's left in the purple gloom. "Damn, that's cold out there," Furuneo said.

"Low temperature and much moisture," the Caleban agreed. McKie, having turned to watch Furuneo enter, saw a closure appear from the solid wall beside the open port. Wind, spray, and surf were shut off.

The temperature in the Ball began to rise.

"It's going to get hot," McKie said.

"What?"

"Hot. Remember the briefings? Calebans like their air hot and dry." He could already feel his damp clothing begin to turn clammy against his skin.

"That's right," Furuneo said. "What's going on?"

"We've been invited in," McKie said. "We didn't disturb him because he has no referent for disturb." He turned back to the spoon shape.

"Where is he?"

"In that spoon thing."

"Yeah . . . I, uh—yeah."

"You may address me as Fanny Mae," the Caleban said. "I can reproduce my kind and answer the equivalents for female."

"Fanny Mae," McKie said with what he knew to be stupid vacuity. *How can you look at the damn thing? Where is its face?* "My companion is Alichino Furuneo, planetary agent on Cordiality for the Bureau of Sabotage." *Fanny Mae? Damn!*

"I make your acquaintance," the Caleban said. "Permit

20

an inquiry into the purpose for your visit.''

Furuneo scratched his right ear. "How're we hearing it?'' He shook his head. "I can understand it, but. . . .''

"Never mind!'' McKie said. And he warned himself: *Gently now. How do you question one of these things?* The insubstantial Caleban presence, the twisting away his mind accepted the thing's words—it all combined with the *angeret* in producing irritation.

"I . . . my orders,'' McKie said. "I seek a Caleban employed by Mliss Abnethe.''

"I receive your questions,'' the Caleban said.

Receive my questions?

McKie tried tipping his head from side to side, wondered if it were possible to achieve an angle of vision where the *something* across from him would assume recognizable substance.

"What're you doing?'' Furuneo asked.

"Trying to see it.''

"You seek visible substance?'' the Caleban asked.

"Uhhh, yes,'' McKie said.

Fanny Mae? he thought. It would be like an original encounter with the Gowachin planets, the first Earth-human encountering the first froglike Gowachin, and the Gowachin introducing himself as William. *Where in ninety thousand worlds did the Caleban dig up that name? And why?*

"I produce mirror,'' the Caleban said, "which reflects outward from projection along plane of being.''

"Are we going to see it?'' Furuneo whispered. "Nobody's ever seen a Caleban.''

"Shhh.''

A half-meter oval *something* of green, blue, and pink without apparent connection to the empty-presence of the Caleban materialized above the giant spoon.

"Think of this as stage upon which I present my selfdom,'' the Caleban said.

"You see anything?'' Furuneo asked.

McKie's visual centers conjured a borderline sensation, a feeling of distant life whose rhythms danced unfleshed within the colorful oval like the sea roaring in an empty shell. He recalled a one-eyed friend and the difficulty of focusing the attention on that lonely eye without being drawn to the vacant

21

patch. *Why couldn't the damn fool just buy a new eye? Why couldn't. . . .*

He swallowed.

"That's the oddest thing I ever saw," Furuneo whispered. "You see it?"

McKie described his visual sensation. "That what you see?"

"I guess so," Furuneo said.

"Visual attempt fails," the Caleban said. "Perhaps I employ insufficient contrast."

Wondering if he could be mistaken, McKie thought he detected a plaintive mood in the Caleban's words. Was it possible Calebans disliked not being seen?

"It's fine," McKie said. "Now, may we discuss the Caleban who . . ."

"Perhaps overlooking cannot be connected," the Caleban said, interrupting. "We enter state for which there exists no remedy. 'As well argue with the night,' as your poets tell us."

The sensation of an enormous sigh swept out from the Caleban and over McKie. It was sadness, a doom-fire gloom. He wondered if they had experienced an *angeret* failure. The emotional strength carried terror within it.

"You feel that?" Furuneo asked.

"Yes."

McKie felt his eyes burning. He blinked. Between blinks, he glimpsed a flower element hovering within the oval—deep red against the room's purple, with black veins woven through it. Slowly it blossomed, closed, blossomed. He wanted to reach out, touch it with a handful of compassion.

"How beautiful," he whispered.

"What is it?" Furuneo whispered.

"I think we're seeing a Caleban."

"I want to cry," Furuneo said.

"Control yourself," McKie cautioned. He cleared his throat. Twanging bits of emotion tumbled through him. They were like pieces cut from the whole and loosed to seek their own patterns. The *angeret* effect was lost in the mixture.

Slowly the image in the oval faded. The emotional torrent subsided.

22

"Wheweee," Furuneo breathed.

"Fanny Mae," McKie ventured. "What was . . ."

"I am one employed by Mliss Abnethe," the Caleban said. "Correct verb usage?"

"Bang!" Furuneo said. "Just like that."

McKie glanced at him, at the place where they had entered the Ball. No sign remained of the oval hole. The heat in the room was becoming unbearable. *Correct verb usage?* He looked at the Caleban manifestation. Something still shimmered above the spoon shape, but it defied his visual centers to describe it.

"Was it asking a question?" Furuneo asked.

"Be still a minute," McKie snapped. "I want to think."

Seconds ticked past. Furuneo felt perspiration running down his neck, under his collar. He could taste it in the corners of his mouth.

McKie sat silently staring at the giant spoon. The Caleban employed by Abnethe. He still felt the aftermath of the emotional mélange. Some lost memory demanded his attention, but he couldn't bring it out for examination.

Furuneo, watching McKie, began to wonder if the Saboteur Extraordinary had been mesmerized. "You still thinking?" he whispered.

McKie nodded, then, "Fanny Mae, where is your employer?"

"Coordinates not permitted," the Caleban said.

"Is she on this planet?"

"Different connectives," the Caleban said.

"I don't think you two are talking the same language," Furuneo said.

"From everything I've read and heard about Calebans, that's the big problem," McKie said. "Communication difficulty."

Furuneo wiped sweat from his forehead. "Have you tried calling Abnethe long distance?" he asked.

"Don't be stupid," McKie said. "That's the first thing I tried."

"Well?"

"Either the Taprisiots are telling the truth and can't make contact, or she's bought them off some way. What difference does it make? So I contact her. How does that tell me where she is? How do I invoke a monitor clause with someone who doesn't wear a monitor?''

"How could she buy off the Taprisiots?"

"How do I know? For that matter, how could she hire a Caleban?"

"Invocation of value exchange," the Caleban said.

McKie chewed at his upper lip.

Furuneo leaned against the wall behind him. He knew what inhibited McKie here. You walked softly with a strange sentient species. No telling what might cause affront. Even the way you phrased a question could cause trouble. They should have assigned a Zeno expert to help McKie. It seemed odd that they hadn't.

"Abnethe offered you something of value, Fanny Mae?" McKie ventured.

"I offer judgment," the Caleban said. "Abnethe may not be judged friendly-good-nice-kindly . . . acceptable."

"Is that . . . your judgment?" McKie asked.

"Your species prohibits flagellation of sentients," the Caleban said. "Fanny Mae orders me flagellated."

"Why don't you . . . just refuse?" McKie asked.

"Contract obligation," the Caleban said.

"Contract obligation." McKie muttered, glancing at Furuneo, who shrugged.

"Ask where she goes to be flagellated," Furuneo said.

"Flagellation comes to me," the Caleban said.

"By flagellation, you mean you're whipped," McKie said.

"Explanation of whipping describes production of froth," the Caleban said. "Not proper term. Abnethe orders me flogged."

"That thing talks like a computer," Furuneo said.

"Let me handle this," McKie ordered.

"Computer describes mechanical device," the Caleban said. "I live."

"He meant no insult," McKie said.

"Insult not interpreted."

"Does the flogging hurt you?" McKie asked.

"Explain hurt."

"Cause you discomfort?"

"Reference recalled. Such sensations explained. Explanations cross no connectives."

Cross no connectives? McKie thought. "Would you choose to be flogged?" he asked.

"Choice made," the Caleban said.

"Well . . . would you make the same choice if you had it to do over?" McKie asked.

"Confusing reference," the Caleban said. "If over refers to repetition, I make no voice in repetition. Abnethe sends Palenki with whip, and flogging occurs."

"A Palenki!" Furuneo said. He shuddered.

"You knew it had to be something like that," McKie said. "What else could you get to do such a thing except a creature without much brain and lots of obedient muscle?"

"But a Palenki! Couldn't we hunt for . . ."

"We've known from the first what she had to be using," McKie said. "Where do you hunt for one Palenki?" He shrugged. "Why can't Calebans understand the concept of being hurt? Is it pure semantics, or do they lack the proper nerve linkages?"

"Understand nerves," the Caleban said. "Any sentience must possess control linkages. But hurt . . . discontinuity of meaning appears insurmountable."

"Abnethe can't stand the sight of pain, you said," Furuneo reminded McKie.

"Yeah. How does she watch the floggings?"

"Abnethe views my home," the Caleban said.

When no further answer was forthcoming, McKie said, "I don't understand. What's that have to do with it?"

"My home this," the Caleban said. "My home contains . . . aligns? Master S'eye. Abnethe possesses connectives for which she pays."

McKie wondered if the Caleban were playing some sarcastic game with him. But all the information about them made no reference to sarcasm. Word confusions, yes, but no apparent insults or subterfuges. Not understand pain, though?

"Abnethe sounds like a mixed-up bitch," McKie muttered.

"Physically unmixed," the Caleban said. "Isolated in her own connectives now, but unified and presentable by your

25

standards—so say judgments made in my presence. If, however, you refer to Abnethe psyche, mixed-up conveys accurate description. What I see of Abnethe psyche most intertwined. Convolutions of odd color displace my vision-sense in extraordinary fashion."

McKie gulped. "You *see* her psyche?"

"I see all psyche."

"So much for the theory that Calebans cannot see," Furuneo said. "All is illusion, eh?"

"How . . . how is this possible?" McKie asked.

"I occupy space between physical and mental," the Caleban said. "Thus your fellow sentients explain in your terminology."

"Gibberish," McKie said.

"You achieve discontinuity of meaning," the Caleban said.

"Why did you accept Abnethe's offer of employment?" McKie asked.

"No common referent for explanation," the Caleban said.

"You achieve discontinuity of meaning," Furuneo said.

"So I surmise," the Caleban said.

"I must find Abnethe," McKie said.

"I give warning," the Caleban said.

"Watch it," Furuneo whispered. "I sense rage that's not connected with the *angeret.*"

McKie waved him to silence. "What warning, Fanny Mae?"

"Potentials in your situation," the Caleban said. "I allow my . . . person? Yes, my person. I allow my person to entrap itself in association which fellow sentients may interpret as non-friendly."

McKie scratched his head, wondered how close they were to anything that could validly be called communication. He wanted to come right out and inquire about the Caleban disappearances, the deaths and insanity, but feared possible consequences.

"Non-friendly," he prompted.

"Understand," the Caleban said, "life which flows in all carries subternal connectives. Each entity remains linked until final discontinuity removes from . . . network? Yes, linkages of other entities into association with Abnethe. Should personal discontinuity overtake self, all entities entangled share it.''

"Discontinuity?" McKie asked, not sure he followed this but afraid he did.

"Tanglements come from contact between sentients not originating in same linearities of awareness," the Caleban said, ignoring McKie's question.

"I'm not sure what you mean by discontinuity," McKie pressed.

"In context," the Caleban said, "ultimate discontinuity, presumed opposite of pleasure—your term."

"You're getting nowhere," Furuneo said. His head ached from trying to equate the radiant impulses of communication from the Caleban with speech.

"Sounds like a semantic identity situation," McKie said. "Black and white statements, but we're trying to find an interpretation in between."

"All between," the Caleban said.

"Presumed opposite of pleasure," McKie muttered.

"Our term," Furuneo reminded him.

"Tell me, Fanny Mae," McKie said, "do we other sentients refer to this *ultimate discontinuity* as death?"

"Presumed approximate term," the Caleban said. "Abnegation of mutual awareness, ultimate discontinuity, death—all appear similar descriptives."

"If you die, many others are going to die, is that it?" McKie asked.

"All users of S'eye. All in tanglement."

"All?" McKie asked, shocked.

"All such in your . . . wave? Di ficult concept. Calebans possess label for this concept . . . plane? Planguinity of beings? Surmise proper term not shared. Problem concealed in visual exclusion which clouds mutual association."

Furuneo touched McKie's arm. "Is she saying that if she dies, everyone who's used a S'eye jumpdoor goes with her?"

"Sounds like it."

"I don't believe it!"

"The evidence would seem to indicate we have to believe her."

27

"But. . . ."

"I wonder if she's in any danger of going soon," McKie mused aloud.

"If you grant the premise, that's a good question," Furuneo said.

"What precedes your ultimate discontinuity, Fanny Mae?" McKie asked.

"All precedes ultimate discontinuity."

"Yeah, but are you headed toward this ultimate discontinuity?"

"Without choice, all head for ultimate discontinuity."

McKie mopped his forehead. The temperature inside the ball had been going up steadily.

"I fulfill demands of honor," the Caleban said. "Acquaint you with prospect. Sentients of your . . . planguinity appear unable, lacking means of withdrawal from influence of my association with Abnethe. Communication understood?"

"McKie," Furuneo said, "have you any idea how many sentients have used a jumpdoor?"

"Damn near everyone."

"Communication understood?" the Caleban repeated.

"I don't now," McKie groaned.

"Difficult sharing of concepts," the Caleban said.

"I still don't believe it," McKie said. "It squares with what some of the other Calebans said, near as we can reconstruct it after the messes they've left."

"Understand withdrawal of companions creates disruption," the Caleban said. "Disruption equates with mess?"

"That's about it," McKie said. "Tell me, Fanny Mae, is there immediate danger of your . . . ultimate discontinuity?"

"Explain imminent," the Caleban said.

"Soon!" McKie snapped. "Short time!"

"Time concept difficult," the Caleban said. "You inquire of personal ability to surmount flagellation?"

"That's good enough," McKie said. "How many more flagellations can you survive?"

"Explain survive," the Caleban said.

"How many flagellations until you experience ultimate

28

discontinuity?'' McKie demanded, fighting down the *angeret*-reinforced frustration.

"Perhaps ten flagellations," the Caleban said. "Perhaps lesser number. Perhaps more."

"And your death will kill all of us?" McKie asked, hoping he'd misunderstood.

"Lesser number than all," the Caleban said.

"You just think you're understanding her," Furuneo said.

"I'm *afraid* I understand her!"

"Fellow Calebans," the Caleban said, "recognizing entrapment, achieve withdrawing. Thus they avoid discontinuity."

"How many Calebans remain in our . . . plane?" McKie asked.

"Single entity of selfness," the Caleban said.

"Just the one," McKie muttered. "That's a damn thin thread!"

"I don't see how the death of one Caleban can cause all that havoc," Furuneo said.

"Explain by comparison," the Caleban said. "Scientist of your planguinity explains reaction of stellar selfdom. Stellar mass enters expanding condition. In this condition, stellar mass engulfs and reduces all substances to other energy patterns. All substances encountered by stellar expansion change. Thus ultimate discontinuity of personal selfdom reaches along linkages of S'eye connectives, repatterns all entities encountered."

"Stellar selfdom," Furuneo said, shaking his head.

"Incorrect term?" the Caleban asked, "Energy selfdom, perhaps."

"She's saying," McKie said, "that use of S'eye doors has tangled us with her life some way. Her death will reach out like a stellar explosion along all these tangled networks and kill us."

"That's what you *think* she's saying," Furuneo objected.

"That's what I have to believe she's saying," McKie said. "Our communication may be tenuous, but I think she's sincere. Can't you still feel the emotions radiating from her?"

"Two species can be said to share emotions only in the

broadest way," Furuneo said. "She doesn't even understand what we mean by pain."

"Scientist of your planguinity," the Caleban said, "Explains emotional base for communication. Lacking emotional commonality, sameness of labels uncertain. Emotion concept not certain for Calebans. Communication difficulty assumed."

McKie nodded to himself. He could see a further complication: the problem of whether the Caleban's words were spoken or radiated in some unthinkable manner completed their confusion.

"I believe you're right in one thing," Furuneo said.

"Yes?"

"We have to assume we understand her."

McKie swallowed in a dry throat. "Fanny Mae," he said, "have you explained this ultimate discontinuity prospect to Mliss Abnethe?"

"Problem explained," the Caleban said. "Fellow Calebans attempt remedy of error. Abnethe fails of comprehension, or disregards consequences. Connectives difficult."

"Connectives difficult," McKie muttered.

"All connectives of single S'eye," the Caleban said. "Master S'eye of self creates mutual problem."

"Don't tell me you understand that," Furuneo objected.

"Abnethe employs Master S'eye of self," the Caleban said. "Contract agreement gives Abnethe right of use. One Master S'eye of self. Abnethe uses."

"So she opens a jumpdoor and sends her Palenki through it," Furuneo said. "Why don't we just wait here and grab her?"

"She could close the door before we even got near her," McKie growled. "No, there's more to what this Caleban's saying. I think she's telling us there's only one Master S'eye, the control system, perhaps, for all the jumpdoors . . . and Fanny Mae here is in control of it, or the channel operation or . . ."

"Or something," Furuneo snarled.

"Abnethe control S'eye by right of purchase," the Caleban said.

"See what I mean?" McKie said. "Can you override her control, Fanny Mae?"

30

"Terms of employment require not interfere."

"But can't you still use your own S'eye doors?" McKie pressed.

"All use," the Caleban said.

"This is insane!" Furuneo snapped.

"Insanity defines as lack of orderly thought progression in mutual acceptance of logical terms," the Caleban said. "Insanity frequent judgment of one species upon other species. Proper interpretation otherwise."

"I think I just had my wrist slapped," Furuneo said.

"Look," McKie said, "the other deaths and insanity around Caleban disappearances substantiate our interpretation. We're dealing with something explosive and dangerous."

"So we find Abnethe and stop her."

"You make that sound so simple," McKie said. "Here are your orders. Get out of here and alert the Bureau. The Caleban's communication won't show on your recorder, but you'll have it all down in your memory. Tell them to scan you for it."

"Right. You're staying?"

"Yes."

"What'll I say you're doing?"

"I want a look at Abnethe's companions and her surroundings."

Furuneo cleared his throat. Gods of the underworld, it was hot! "Have you thought of, you know, just bang?" He made the motion of firing a raygen.

"There's a limit on what can go through a jumpdoor and how fast," McKie chided. "You know that."

"Maybe this jumpdoor's different."

"I doubt it."

"After I've reported in, what then?"

"Sit tight outside there until I call you—unless they give you a message for me. Oh, and start a general search on Cordiality . . . just in case."

"Of course." Furuneo hesitated. "One thing—who do I contact at the Bureau? Bildoon?"

McKie glanced up. Why should Furuneo question whom to call? What was he trying to say?

It dawned on McKie then that Furuneo had hit on a logical

31

concern. BuSab director Napoleon Bildoon was a Pan Spechi, a pentarchal sentient, human only in appearance. Since McKie, a human, held nominal charge of this case, that might appear to confine control of it, excluding other members of the ConSentiency. Interspecies political infighting could take odd turns in a time of stress. It would be best to involve a broad directorate here.

"Thanks," McKie said. "I wasn't thinking much beyond the immediate problem."

"This *is* the immediate problem."

"I understand. All right, I was tapped for this chore by our Director of Discretion."

"Gitchel Siker?"

"Yes."

"That's one Laclac and Bildoon, a Pan Spechi. Who else?"

"Get somebody out of the Legal Department."

"Bound to be a human."

"The minute you stretch it that far, they'll all get the message," McKie said. "They'll bring in the others before making any official decision."

Furuneo nodded. "One other thing."

"What?"

"How do I get out of here?"

McKie faced the giant spoon. "Good question. Fanny Mae, how does my companion leave here?"

"He wishes to journey where?"

"To his home."

"Connectives apparent," the Caleban said.

McKie felt a gush of air. His ears popped to a change in pressure. There was a sound like the pulling of a cork from a bottle. He whirled. Furuneo was gone.

"You . . . sent him home?" McKie asked.

"Correct," the Caleban said. "Desired destination visible. Sent swiftness. Prevent temperature drop below proper level."

McKie, feeling perspiration roll down his cheeks, said, "I wish I knew how you did that. Can you actually *see* our thoughts?"

"See only strong connectives," the Caleban said.

Discontinuity of meaning, McKie thought.

The Caleban's remark about temperature came back to him. What was a proper temperature level? Damn! It was boiling in here! His skin itched with perspiration. His throat was dry. Proper temperature level?

"What's the opposite of proper?" he asked.

"False," the Caleban said.

The play of words can lead to certain expectations which life is unable to match. This is a source of much insanity and other forms of unhappiness.

—Wreave Saying

For a reflexive time which he found himself unable to measure, McKie considered his exchange with the Caleban. He felt cast adrift without any familiar reference points. How could *false* be the opposite of *proper?* If he could not measure meanings, how could he measure time?

McKie passed a hand across his forehead, gathering perspiration which he tried to wipe off on his jacket. The jacket was damp.

No matter how much time had passed, he felt that he still knew where he *was* in this universe. The beachball's interior walls remained around him. The *unseeable* presence of the Caleban had not become less mysterious, but he could look at the shimmering existence of the thing and take a certain satisfaction from the fact that it spoke to him.

The thought that every sentient who had used a jumpdoor would die if this Caleban succumbed sat on McKie's awareness. It was muscle-numbing. His skin was slick with perspiration, and not all of it from the heat. There were voices of death in this air. He thought of himself as a being surrounded by all those pleading sentients—quadrillions upon quadrillions of them. *Help us!*

Everyone who'd used a jumpdoor.

Damnation of all devils! Had he interpreted the Caleban correctly? It was the logical assumption. Deaths and insanity around the Caleban *disappearances* said he must exclude any other interpretation.

Link by link, this trap had been forged. It would crowd the universe with dead flesh.

The shimmering oval above the giant spoon abruptly

waved outward, contracted, flowed up, down, left. McKie received a definite impression of distress. The oval vanished, but his eyes still tracked the Caleban's *unpresence.*

"Is something wrong?" McKie asked.

For answer the round vortal tube of a S'eye jumpdoor opened behind the Caleban. Beyond the opening stood a woman, a figure dwarfed as though seen through the wrong end of a telescope. McKie recognized her from all the news-visos and from the holoscans he had been fed as background briefing for this assignment.

He was confronting Mliss Abnethe in a light somewhat reddened by its slowed passage through the jumpdoor.

It was obvious that the Beautybarbers of Steadyon had been about their expensive work on her person. He made a mental note to have that checked. Her figure presented the youthful curves of a pleasurefem. The face beneath fairy-blue hair was focused around a red-petal mouth. Large sum-mery green eyes and a sharply cleaving nose conveyed odd contrast—dignity versus hoyden. She was a flawed queen, age mingled with youth. She must be at least eighty standard years, but the Beautybarbers had achieved this startling combination: available pleasurefem and remote, hungry power.

The expensive body wore a long gown of grey rainpearls which matched her, movement for movement, like a glitter-ing skin. She moved nearer the vortal tube. As she ap-proached, the edges of the tube blocked off first her feet, then her legs, thighs, waist.

McKie felt his knees age a thousand years in that brief passage. He remained crouched near the place where he'd entered the Beachball.

"Ahhh, Fanny Mae," Mliss Abnethe said. "You have a guest." Jumpdoor interference caused her voice to sound faintly hoarse.

"I am Jorj X. McKie, Saboteur Extraordinary," he said.

Was that a contraction in the pupils of her eyes? McKie wondered. She stopped with only her head and shoulders visible in the tube's circle.

"And *I* am Mliss Abnethe, private citizen."

Private citizen! McKie thought. This bitch controlled the

productive capacity of at least five hundred worlds. Slowly McKie got to his feet.

"The Bureau of Sabotage has official business with you," he said, putting her on notice to satisfy the legalities.

"I am a *private* citizen!" she barked. The voice was prideful, vain, marred by petulance.

McKie took heart at the revealed weakness. It was a particular kind of flaw that often went with wealth and power. He had had experience in dealing with such flaws.

"Fanny Mae, am I your guest?" he asked.

"Indeed," the Caleban said. "I open my door to you."

"Am I your employer, Fanny Mae?" Abnethe demanded.

"Indeed, you employ me."

A breathless, crouching look came over her face. Her eyes went to slits. "Very well. Then prepare to fulfill the obligations of . . ."

"One moment!" McKie said. He felt desperate. Why was she moving so fast? What was that faint whine in her voice? "Guests do not interfere," Abnethe said.

"BuSab makes its own decisions about interference!" McKie said.

"Your jurisdiction has limits!" she countered.

McKie heard the beginnings of many actions in that statement: hired operatives, gigantic sums spent as bribes, doctored agreements, treaties, stories planted with the visos on how this good and proud lady had been mistreated by her government, a wide enlistment of personal concern to justify—what? Violence against his person? He thought not. More likely to discredit him, to saddle him with onerous misdeeds.

Thought of all that power made McKie wonder suddenly why he made himself vulnerable to it. Why had he chosen BuSab? *Because I'm difficult to please,* he told himself. *I'm a Saboteur by choice.* There was no going back on that choice now. BuSab appeared to walk down the middle of everywhere and always wound up on the high road.

And this time BuSab appeared to be carrying most of the sentient universe on its shoulders. It was a fragile burden perched there, fearful and feared. It had sunk stark claws into him.

"Agreed, we have limits," McKie growled, "but I doubt you'll ever see them. Now, what's going on here?"

"You're not a police agent!" Abnethe barked.

"Perhaps I should summon police," McKie said.

"On what grounds?" She smiled. She had him there and knew it. Her legal staff had explained to her the open association clause in the ConSentient Articles of Federation: *"When members of different species agree formally to an association from which they derive mutual benefits, the contracting parties shall be the sole judges of said benefits, providing their agreement breaks no law, covenant, or legative article binding upon said contracting parties; provided further that said formal agreement was achieved by voluntary means and involves no breach of the public peace."*

"Your actions will bring about the death of this Caleban," McKie said. He didn't hold out much hope for this argument, but it bought a bit more time.

"You'll have to establish that the Caleban concept of discontinuity interprets precisely as death," Abnethe said. "You can't do that, because it's not true. Why do you interfere? This is just harmless play between consenting ad—"

"More than play," the Caleban said.

"Fanny Mae!" Abnethe snapped. "You are *not* to interrupt! Remember our agreement."

McKie stared in the direction of the Caleban's *unpresence,* tried to interpret the spectrum-flare that rejected his senses.

"Discern conflict between ideals and structure of government," the Caleban said.

"Precisely!" Abnethe said. "I'm assured that Calebans cannot suffer pain, that they don't even have a term for it. If it's my pleasure to stage an apparent flogging and observe the reactions of . . ."

"Are you sure she suffers no pain?" McKie asked.

Again a gloating smile came over Abnethe's face. "I've never seen her suffer pain. Have you?"

"Have you seen her do anything?"

"I've seen her come and go."

"Do you suffer pain, Fanny Mae?" McKie asked.

37

"No referents for this concept," the Caleban said.

"Are these floggings going to bring about your ultimate discontinuity?" McKie asked.

"Explain bring about," the Caleban said.

"Is there any connection between the floggings and your ultimate discontinuity?"

"Total universe connectives include all events," the Caleban said.

"I pay well for my game," Abnethe said. "Stop interfering, McKie."

"How're you paying?"

"None of your business!"

"I make it my business," McKie said. "Fanny Mae?"

"Don't answer him!" Abnethe snapped.

"I can still summon police and the officers of a Discretionary Court," McKie said.

"By all means," Abnethe gloated. "You are, of course, ready to answer a suit charging interference with an open agreement between consenting members of different species?"

"I can still get an injunction," McKie said. "What's your present address?"

"I decline to answer on advice of counsel."

McKie glared at her. She had him. He could not charge her with flight to prevent prosecution unless he had proved a crime. To prove a crime he must get a court to act and serve her with the proper papers in the presence of bonded witnesses, bring her into a court, and allow her to face her accusers. And her attorneys would tie him in knots every step of the way.

"Offer judgment," the Caleban said. "Nothing in Abnethe contract prohibits revelation of payment. Employer provides educators."

"Educators?" McKie asked.

"Very well," Abnethe conceded. "I provide Fanny Mae with the finest instructors and teaching aids our civilization can supply. She's been soaking up our culture. Anything she requested, she's got. And it wasn't cheap."

"And she still doesn't understand pain?" McKie demanded.

38

"Hope to acquire proper referents," the Caleban said.

"Will you have time to acquire those referents?" McKie asked.

"Time difficult concept," the Caleban said. "Statement of instructor, to wit: 'Relevancy of time to learning varies with species.' Time possesses length, unknown quality termed duration, subjective and objective dimension. Confusing."

"Let's make this official," McKie said. "Abnethe, are you aware that you're killing this Caleban?"

"Discontinuity and death are not the same," Abnethe objected. "Are they, Fanny Mae?"

"Wide disparity of equivalents exists between separate waves of being," the Caleban said.

"I ask you formally, Mliss Abnethe," McKie said, "if this Caleban calling herself Fanny Mae has told you the consequences of an event she describes as ultimate discontinuity."

"You just heard her say there are no equivalents!"

"You've not answered my question."

"You're quibbling!"

"Fanny Mae," McKie said, "have you described for Mliss Abnethe the consequences of . . ."

"Bound by contract connectives," the Caleban said.

"You see!" Abnethe pounced. "She's bound by our open agreement, and you're interfering." Abnethe gestured to someone not visible in the jumpdoor's vortal tube.

The opening suddenly doubled its diameter. Abnethe stepped aside, leaving half her head and one eye visible to McKie. A crowd of watching sentients could now be discerned in the background. Into Abnethe's place darted the turtle form of a giant Palenki. Its hundreds of tiny feet flickered beneath its bulk. The single arm growing from the top of its ring-eyed head trailed a long whip in a double-thumbed hand. The arm thrust through the tube, jerked the whip against jumpdoor resistance, lashed the whip forward. The whip cracked above the spoon bowl.

A crystalline spray of green showered the unseeable region of the Caleban. It glittered for a moment like a fluorescent explosion of fireworks, dissolved.

An ecstatic moan came through the vortal tube.

McKie fought an intense outpouring sensation of distress, leaped forward. Instantly, the S'eye jumpdoor closed, dumping a severed Palenki arm and whip onto the floor of the room. The arm writhed and turned, slower . . . slower. It fell still.

"Fanny Mae?" McKie said.

"Yes?"

"Did that whip hit you?"

"Explain whip hit."

"Encounter your substance!"

"Approximately."

McKie moved close to the spoon bowl. He still sensed distress but knew it could be a side effect of *angeret* and the incident he had just witnessed.

"Describe the flogging sensation," he said.

"You possess no proper referents."

"Try me."

"I inhaled substance of whip, exhaled my own substance."

"You breathed it?"

"Approximately."

"Well . . . describe your physical reactions."

"No common physical referents."

"Any reaction, dammit!"

"Whip incompatible with my glssrrk."

"Your what?"

"No common referents."

"What was that green spray when it hit you?"

"Explain greenspray."

By referring to wavelengths and describing airborne water droplets, with a side excursion into wave and wind action, McKie thought he conveyed an approximate idea of green spray.

"You observe this phenomenon?" the Caleban asked.

"I saw it, yes."

"Extraordinary!"

McKie hesitated, an odd thought filling his mind. *Could we be as insubstantial to Calebans as they appear to us?*

He asked.

40

"All creatures possess substance relative to their own quantum existence," the Caleban said.

"But do you see our substance when you look at us?"

"Basic difficulty. Your species repeats this question. Possess no certain answer."

"Try to explain. Start by telling me about the green spray."

"Greenspray unknown phenomenon."

"But what could it be?"

"Perhaps interplanar phenomenon, reaction to exhalation of my substance."

"Is there a limit of how much of your substance you can exhale?"

"Quantum relationship defines limitations of your plane. Movement exists between planar origins. Movement changes referential relatives."

No constant referents? McKie wondered. But there had to be! He explored this aspect with the Caleban, questions and answers obviously making less and less sense to both of them.

"But there must be some constant!" McKie exploded.

"Connectives possess aspect of this constant you seek," the Caleban said.

"What are connectives?"

"No . . ."

"Referents!" McKie stormed. "Then why use the term?"

"Term approximates. Tangential occlusion another term expression something similar."

"Tangential occlusion," McKie muttered. Then, "tangential occlusion?"

"Fellow Caleban offers this term after discussion of problem with Laclac sentient possessing rare insight."

"One of you talked this over with a Laclac, eh? Who was this Laclac?"

"Identity not conveyed, but occupation known and understandable."

"Oh? What was his occupation?"

"Dentist."

McKie exhaled a long, held breath, shook his head with bewilderment. "You understand—dentist?"

41

"All species requiring ingestion of energy sources must reduce such sources to convenient form."

"You mean they bite?" McKie asked.

"Explain bite."

"I thought you understood dentist!"

"Dentist—one who maintains system by which sentients shape energy for ingestion," the Caleban said.

"Tangential occlusion," McKie muttered. "Explain what you understand by occlusion."

"Proper matching of related parts in shaping system."

"We're getting nowhere," McKie growled.

"Every creature somewhere," the Caleban said.

"But where? Where are you, for example?"

"Planar relationships unexplainable."

"Let's try something else," McKie said. "I've heard you can read our writing."

"Reducing what you term writing to compatible connectives suggests time-constant communication," the Caleban said. "Not really certain, however, of time-constant or required connectives."

"Well . . . let's go at the verb *to see,*" McKie said. "Tell me what you understand by the action of seeing."

"To see—receive sensory awareness of external energy," the Caleban said.

McKie buried his face in his hands. He felt dispirited, his brain numbed by the Caleban's radiant bombardment. What would be the sensory organs? He knew such a question would only send them off on another empty label chase.

He might as well be listening to all this with his eyes or with some other organ rude and unfitted to its task. Too much depended on what he did. McKie's imagination sensed the stillness which would follow the death of this Caleban—an enormous solitude. A few infants left, perhaps—but doomed. All the good, the beautiful, the evil . . . everything sentient . . . all gone. Dumb creatures which had never gone through a jumpdoor would remain. And winds, colors, floral perfumes, birdsong—these would continue after the crystal shattering of sentiency.

But the dreams would be gone, lost in that season of death. There would be a special kind of silence: no more beautiful speech strewn with arrows of meaning.

42

Who could console the universe for such a loss?

Presently he dropped his hands, said, "Is there *somewhere* you could take this . . . your *home* where Mliss Abnethe couldn't reach you?"

"Withdrawal possible."

"Well, do it!"

"Cannot."

"Why?"

"Agreement prohibits."

"Break the damned agreement!"

"Dishonorable action brings ultimate discontinuity for all sentients on your . . . suggest *wave* as preferred term. Wave. Much closer than plane. Please substitute concept of wave wherever plane used in our discussion."

This thing's impossible, McKie thought.

He lifted his arms in a gesture of frustration and, in the movement, felt his body jerk as a long-distance call ignited his pineal gland. The message began to roll, and he knew his body had gone into the sniggertrance, mumbling and chuckling, trembling occasionally.

But this time he didn't resent the call.

All definitions, no matter the language, should be considered probationary.

> —The Caleban Question
> by Dwel Hartavid

"Gitchel Siker here," the caller said.

McKie imagined the Bureau's Director of Discretion, a suave little Laclac sitting in that nicely tailored environment back at Central. Siker would be relaxed, fighting tendril withdrawn, his face split open, an elite chairdog ministering to his flesh, trained minions a button-push away.

"About time you called," McKie said.

"About time *I* called?"

"Well, you certainly must've gotten Furuneo's message quite a . . ."

"What message?"

McKie felt as though his mind had touched a grinding wheel shooting off ideas like sparks. No message from Furuneo?

"Furuneo," McKie said, "left here long enough ago to . . ."

"I'm calling," Siker interrupted, "because there's been no sign of either of you for too damn long, and Furuneo's enforcers are worried. One of them . . . Where was Furuneo supposed to go and how?"

McKie felt an idea blossoming in his mind. "Where was Furuneo born?"

"Born? On Landy-B. Why?"

"I think we'll find him there. The Caleban used its S'eye system to send him *home*. If he hasn't called yet, better send for him. He was supposed to . . ."

"Landy-B only has three Taprisiots and one jumpdoor. It's a retreat planet, full of recluses and . . ."

"That'd explain the delay. Meanwhile, here's the situation. . . ."

44

McKie began detailing the problem.

"Do you believe this, this *ultimate discontinuity* thing?" Siker interrupted.

"We have to believe it. The evidence all says it's true."

"Well, maybe . . . but . . ."

"Can we afford a *maybe,* Siker?"

"We'd better call in the police."

"I think she wants us to do just that."

"Wants us. . . . Why?"

"Who'd have to sign a complaint?"

Silence.

"Are you getting the picture?" McKie pressed.

"It's on your head, McKie."

"It always is. But if we're right, that doesn't make any difference, does it?"

"I'm going to suggest," Siker said, "that we contact the top level in the Central Police Bureau—for consultation only. Agreed?"

"Discuss that with Bildoon. Meanwhile, here's what I want done. Assemble a Bureau ConSentient Council, draft another max-alert message. Keep the emphasis on Calebans, but bring in the Palenkis, and start looking into Abnethe's . . ."

"We can't do that, and you know it!"

"We have to do it."

"When you took this assignment, you received a full explanation of why we . . ."

"Utmost discretion doesn't mean hands off," McKie said. "If that's the way you're thinking, then you've missed the importance of . . ."

"McKie, I can't believe . . ."

"Sing off, Siker," McKie said. "I'm going over your head to Bildoon."

Silence.

"Break his contact!" McKie ordered.

"That won't be necessary."

"Won't it?"

"I'll put the agents onto Abnethe at once. I see your point. If we assume that . . ."

"We assume," McKie said.

45

"The orders will be issued in your name, of course," Siker said.

"Keep your skirts clean any way you like," McKie said. "Now, have our people start probing into the Beautybarbers of Steadyon. She's been there, and recently. Also, I'll be sending along a whip she . . ."

"A whip?"

"I just witnessed one of the flagellations. Abnethe cut the connection while her Palenki still had an arm through the S'eye door. Cut the arm right off. The Palenki will grow another arm, and she can hire more Palenkis, but the whip and arm could give us a lead. Palenkis don't practice gene tagging, I know, but it's the best we have at the moment."

"I understand. What'd you see during the . . . incident?"

"I'm getting to that."

"Hadn't you better come in and put your report directly onto a transcorder?"

"I'll depend on you for that. Don't think I should show at Central for a bit."

"Mmm. See what you mean. She'll try to tie you up with a countersuit."

"Or I miss my guess. Now, here's what I saw. When she opened the door, she practically filled it, but I could see what appeared to be a window in the background. If it was a window, it opened onto a cloudy sky. That means daylight."

"Cloudy?"

"Yes. Why?"

"It's been cloudy here all morning."

"You don't think she's . . . no, she wouldn't."

"Probably not, but we'll have Central scoured just to be sure. With her money, no telling who she might've bought."

"Yeah . . . well, the Palenki. Its shell carried an odd design—triangles, diamonds in red and orange, and a rope or snake of yellow wound all the way around and through it."

"Phylum identification," Siker said.

"Yes, but what Palenki family?"

"Well, we'll check it. What else?"

"There was a mob of sentients behind her during the actual flogging. I saw Preylings, couldn't miss those wire tentacles. There were some Chithers, a few Soborips, some Wreaves . . ."

"Sounds like her usual patch of sycophants. Recognize any of them?"

"I'll try for ID's later, but I couldn't attach any names to this mob. But there was one, a Pan Spechi, and he was stage-frozen or I miss my guess."

"You sure?"

"All I know is what I saw, and I saw the scars on his forehead—ego surgery, sure as I'm sniggering."

"That's against every Pan Spechi legal, moral, and ethical . . ."

"The scars were purple," McKie said. "That checks, doesn't it?"

"Right out in the open, no makeup or anything to cover the scars?"

"Nothing. If I'm right, it means he's the only Pan Spechi with her. Another would kill him on sight."

"Where could she be where there'd be only one Pan Spechi?"

"Beats me. Oh, and there were some humans, too—green uniforms."

"Abnethe house guards."

"That's the way I made it."

"Quite a mob to be hiding away."

"If anyone can afford it, she can."

"One more thing," McKie said. "I smelled yeast."

"Yeast?"

"No doubt about it. There's always a pressure differential through a jumpdoor. It was blowing our way. Yeast."

"That's quite a bag of observations."

"Did you think I was getting careless?"

"No more than usual. Are you absolutely sure about that Pan Spechi?"

"I saw the eyes."

"Sunken, the facets smoothing over?"

"That's the way it looked to me."

"If we can get a Pan Spechi to make an official observation of this fellow, that'd give us a lever. Harboring a criminal, you know."

"Apparently, you haven't much experience with Pan Spechi," McKie said. "How'd you get to be Director of Discretion?"

"All right, McKie, let's not . . ."

"You know damn well a Pan Spechi would blow up if he saw this fellow. Our observer would try to dive through the jumpdoor and . . ."

"So?"

"Abnethe would close it on him. She'd have half of our observer, and we'd have the other half."

"But that'd be murder!"

"An unfortunate accident, no more."

"That woman *does* swing a lot of weight, I admit, but . . ."

"And she'll have our hides if she can make it stick that she's a private citizen and we're trying to sabotage her."

"Messy," Siker agreed. "I hope you made no official sounds in her direction."

"Ah, but I did."

"You what?"

"I put her on official notice."

"McKie, you were told to handle this with dis—"

"Look, we want her to start official action. Check with Legal. She can try a countersuit against me personally, but if she moves against the Bureau, we can ask for a *seratori* hearing, a personal confrontation. Her legal staff will advise her of that. No, she'll try to get at . . ."

"She may not go into court against the Bureau," Siker said, "but she's certain to set her dogs on us. And it couldn't come at a worse time. Bildoon has just about used up his ego-time. He'll be going into the crèche any time now. You know what that means."

"The Bureau Director's chair up for grabs," McKie said. "I've been expecting it."

"Yes, but things'll be in a real uproar around here."

"You're eligible for the seat, Siker."

"So are you, McKie."

"I pass."

"That'll be the day! What I'm worried about is Bildoon. He'll blow when he hears about this ego-frozen Pan Spechi. That might be all it takes to . . ."

48

"He'll handle it," McKie said, putting more confidence into the statement than he felt.

"And you could be wrong. I hope you know I'm not passing."

"We all know you want the job," McKie said.

"I can imagine the gossip."

"Is it worth it?"

"I'll let you know."

"I'm sure you will."

"One thing," Siker said. "How're you going to keep Abnethe off your back?"

"I'm going to become a schoolteacher," McKie said.

"I don't think I want that explained," Siker said. He broke the contact.

McKie found himself still seated in the purple gloom of the Beachball. Sweat bathed his body. The place was an oven. He wondered if his fat was actually being reduced by the heat. Water loss, certainly. The instant he thought of water, he sensed the dryness in his throat.

"You still there?" he rasped.

Silence.

"Fanny Mae?"

"I remain in my home," the Caleban said.

The sensation that he heard the words without hearing grated on McKie, fed on the *angeret* in his system, stirred a latent rage. *Damn superior stupid Caleban! Got us into a real mess!*

"Are you willing to cooperate with us in trying to stop these floggings?" McKie asked.

"As my contract permits."

"All right. Then you insist to Abenethe that you want me as your teacher."

"You perform functions of teacher?"

"Have you learned anything from me?" McKie asked.

"All mingled connectives instruct."

"Connectives," McKie muttered. "I must be getting old."

"Explain old," the Caleban said.

"Never mind. We should've discussed your contract first thing. Maybe there's a way to break it. Under what laws was it executed?"

"Explain laws."

"What honorable system of enforcement?" McKie blared.

"Under natural honor of sentient connectives."

"Abnethe doesn't know what honor means."

"I understand honor."

McKie sighed. "Were there witnesses, signatures, that sort of thing?"

"All my fellow Calebans witness connectives. Signatures not understood. Explain."

McKie decided not to explore the concept of signatures. Instead he asked, "Under what circumstances could you refuse to honor your contract with Abnethe?"

After a prolonged pause the Caleban said, "Changing circumstances convey variable relationships. Should Abnethe fail in her connectives or attempt redefinition of essences, this could produce linearities open for my disentanglement."

"Sure," McKie said. "That figures."

He shook his head, studied the empty air above the giant spoon. Calebans! You couldn't see them, couldn't hear them, couldn't understand them.

"Is the use of your S'eye system available to me?" McKie asked.

"You function as my teacher."

"Is that a yes?"

"Affirmative answer."

"Affirmative answer," McKie echoed. "Fine. Can you also transport objects to me, sending them where I direct?"

"While connectives remain apparent."

"I hope that means what I think it does," McKie said. "Are you aware of the Palenki arm and whip over there on your floor?"

"Aware."

"I want them sent to a particular office at Central. Can you do that?"

"Think of office," the Caleban said.

McKie obeyed.

"Connectives available," the Caleban said. "You desire sending to place of examination."

50

"That's right!"

"Send now?"

"At once."

"Once, yes. Multiple sending remains outside our capabilities."

"Huh?"

"Objects going."

As McKie blinked, the arm and whip snapped out of his view accompanied by a sharp crack of exploding air.

"Do the Taprisiots work in any way similar to what you do transporting things?" McKie asked.

"Message transportation minor energy level," the Caleban said. "Beautybarbers even more minor."

"I guess so," McKie said. "Well, never mind. There's the little matter of my friend, Alichino Furuneo, though. You sent him home, I believe?"

"Correct."

"You sent him to the wrong home."

"Creatures possess only one home."

"We sentients have more than one home."

"But I view connectives!"

McKie felt the wash of radiant objection from the Caleban, steadied himself. "No doubt," he said. "But he has another home right here on Cordiality."

"Astonishment fills me."

"Probably. The question remains, can you correct this situation?"

"Explain situation."

"Can you send him to his home on Cordiality?"

Pause then, "That place not his home."

"But can you send him there?"

"You wish this?"

"I wish it."

"Your friend converses through a Taprisiot."

"Ahhh," McKie said. "You can listen in on his conversation, then?"

"Message content not available. Connectives visible. I possess awareness that your friend exchanges communication with sentient of other species."

"What species?"

"One you label Pan Spechi."

"What'd happen if you sent Furuneo to . . . his home here on Cordiality right now?"

"Shattering of connectives. But message exchange concludes in this linearity. I send him. There."

"You sent him?"

"But connectives you convey."

"He's here on Cordiality right now?"

"He occupies place not his home."

"I hope we're together on that."

"Your friend," the Caleban said, "desires presence with you."

"He wants to come here?"

"Correct."

"Well, why not? All right, bring him."

"What purpose arises from friend's presence in my home?"

"I want him to stay with you and watch for Abnethe while I attend to other business."

"McKie?"

"Yes."

"You possess awareness that presence of yourself or other of your kind prolongs impingement of myself upon your wave?"

"That's fine."

"Your presence foreshortens flogging."

"I suspected as much."

"Suspected?"

"I understand!"

"Understanding probable. Connectives indicative."

"I can't tell you how happy that makes me," McKie said.

"You wish friend brought?"

"What's Furuneo doing?"

"Furuneo exchanges communication with . . . assistant."

"I can imagine."

McKie shook his head from side to side. He could sense the morass of misunderstanding around every attempt at communication here. No way to steer clear of it. No way at all. At the very moment when they thought they had achieved closest communication, right then they could be widest of the mark.

"When Furuneo concludes his conversation, bring him,"

McKie said. He hunched back against the wall. Gods of the underworld! The heat was almost unbearable. Why did Calebans require such heat? Maybe the heat represented something else to a Caleban, a visible wave form, perhaps, serving some function other sentients couldn't begin to understand.

McKie felt then that he was engaged in an exchange of worthless noises here—shadow sounds. Reason had gone, swinging from planet to planet. He and the Caleban were striking false bargains, trying to climb out of chaos. If they failed, death would take away all the innocent and the sinful, the good and the guilty. Boats would drift on countless oceans, towers would fall, balconies crumble, and suns would move alone across unmarked skies.

A wave of relatively cold air told McKie that Furuneo had arrived. McKie turned, saw the planetary agent sprawled beside him and just beginning to sit up.

"For the love of reason!" Furuneo shouted. "What're you doing to me?"

"I needed the fresh air," McKie said.

Furuneo peered at him. "What?"

"Glad to see you," McKie said.

"Yeah?" Furuneo brought himself to a squatting position beside McKie. "You have any idea what's just happened to me?"

"You've been to Landy-B," McKie said.

"How'd you know? Was that your doing?"

"Slight misunderstanding," McKie said. "Landy-B's your home."

"It is not!"

"I'll leave you to argue that with Fanny Mae," McKie said. "Have you started the search on Cordiality?"

"I barely got it going before you . . ."

"Yes, but you've started it?"

"I've started it."

"Good. Fanny Mae will keep you posted on various things and bring your people here for reports and such as you need them. Won't you, Fanny Mae?"

"Connectives remain available. Contract permits."

"Good girl."

"I'd almost forgotten how hot it was in here," Furuneo

53

said, mopping his forehead. "So I can summon people. What else?"

"You watch for Abnethe."

"And?"

"The instant she and one of her Palenki floggers make an appearance, you get a holoscan record of everything that happens. You do have your toolkit?"

"Of course."

"Fine. While you're scanning, get your instruments as close to the jumpdoor as you can."

"She'll probably close the door as soon as she sees what I'm doing."

"Don't count on it. Oh, one thing."

"Yes?"

"You're my teaching assistant."

"Your what?"

McKie explained about the Caleban's agreement.

"So she can't get rid of us without violating the terms of her contract with Fanny Mae," Furuneo said. "Cute." He pursed his lips. "That all?"

"No. I want you and Fanny Mae to discuss connectives."

"Connectives?"

"Connectives. I want you to try finding out what in ten billion devils a Caleban means by connectives."

"Connectives," Furuneo said. "Is there any way to turn down the furnace in here?"

"You might take that as another subject: Try to discover the reason for all this heat."

"If I don't melt first. Where'll you be?"

"Hunting—provided Fanny Mae and I can agree on the connectives."

"You're not making sense."

"Right. But I'll try to make tracks—if Fanny Mae'll send me where the game is."

"Ahhh," Furuneo said. "You could walk into a trap."

"Maybe. Fanny Mae, have you been listening?"

"Explain listening."

"Never mind!"

"But mind possesses ever!"

McKie closed his eyes, swallowed, then, "Fanny Mae,

are you aware of the information exchange just concluded between my friend and myself here?''

"Explain conclu . . ."

"Are you aware?" McKie bellowed.

"Amplification contributes little to communication," the Caleban said. "I possess desired awareness—presumably."

"Presumably," McKie muttered, then, "Can you send me to a place near Abnethe where she will not be aware of me, but where I can be aware of her?"

"Negative."

"Why not?"

"Specific injunction of contract."

"Oh." McKie bent his head in thought, then, "Well, can you send me to a place where I might become aware of Abnethe through my own efforts?"

"Possibility. Permit examination of connectives."

McKie waited. The heat was a tangible thing inside the Beachball, a solid intrusion on his senses. He saw it was already beginning to wilt Furuneo.

"I saw my mother," Furuneo said, noting McKie's attention.

"That's great," McKie said.

"She was swimming with friends when the Caleban dumped me right in the pool with them. The water was wonderful."

"They were surprised, no doubt."

"They thought it was a great joke. I wish I knew how that S'eye system works."

"You and a billion billion others. The energy requirement gives me the chills."

"I could use a chill right now. You know, that's one weird sensation—standing one minute talking to old friends, the next instant yakking at empty air here on Cordiality. What do you suppose they think?"

"They think it's magic."

"McKie," the Caleban said, "I love you."

"You what?" McKie exploded.

"Love you," the Caleban repeated. "Affinity of one person for another person. Such affinity transcends species."

"I guess so, but . . . ."

"Since I possess this universal affinity for your person, connectives open, permitting accomplishment of your request."

"You can send me to a place near Abnethe?"

"Affirmative. Accord with desire. Yes."

"Where is this place?" McKie asked.

He found, with a chill wash of air and a sprawling lurch onto dusty ground, that he was addressing his question to a moss-capped rock. For a moment he stared at the rock, regaining his balance. The rock was about a meter tall and contained small veins of yellow-white quartz with flecks of reflective brilliance scattered through them. It stood in an open meadow beneath a distant yellow sun. The sun's position told McKie he'd arrived either at midmorning or mid-afternoon local.

Beyond the rock, the meadow, and a ring of straggly yellow brushes stretched a flat horizon broken by the tall white spires of a city.

"Loves me?" he asked the rock.

Whip and severed Palenki arm arrived at the proper BuSab laboratory while it was temporarily unoccupied. The lab chief, a Bureau veteran named Treej Tuluk, a back-bowing Wreave, was away at the time, attending the conference which McKie's report had precipitated.

As with most back-bowers, Tuluk was an odor-id Wreave. He had an average-appearing Wreave body, two and a half meters tall, tubular, pedal bifurcation, vertical face slit with manipulative extensors dangling from the lower corner. From long association with humans and humanoids he had developed a brisk, slouching gait, a predilection for clothing with pockets, and un-Wreavish speech mannerisms of a cynical tone. The four eye tubes protruding from the top of his facial slit were green and mild.

Returning from the conference, he recognized the objects on his lab floor immediately. They matched Siker's description. Tuluk complained to himself briefly about the careless manner of delivery and was soon lost in the intricacies of examination. He and the assistants he summoned made initial holoscans before separating whip and arm.

As they had expected, the Palenki gene structure offered no comparatives. The arm had not come from one of the few Palenkis on record in the ConSentient Register. Tuluk filed the DNA chart and message sequence, however. These could be used to identify the arm's original owner, if that became necessary.

At the same time study of the whip went ahead. The artifact report came out of the computers as "Bullwhip, copy of ancient earth type." It was made of steerhide, a fact which gave Tuluk and his vegetarian aides a few brief moments of disgust, since they had assumed it was a synthetic.

"A sick archaism," one of Tuluk's Chither assistants called the whip. The others agreed with this judgment, even a Pan Spechi for whom periodic reversion to carnivorous type in his crèche cycle was necessary to survival.

A curious alignment in some of the cell molecules attracted their attention then. Study of whip and arm continued at their respective paces.

There is no such thing as pure objectivity.

—Gowachin Aphorism

McKie took the long-distance call while standing beside a dirt road about three kilometers from the rock. He had come this far on foot, increasingly annoyed by the strange surroundings. The city, he had soon discovered, was a mirage hanging over a dusty plain of tall grass and scrubby thornbushes.

It was almost as hot on the plain as it had been in the Caleban's Beachball.

Thus far the only living things he had seen were some distant tawny animals and countless insects—leapers, crawlers, fliers, hoppers. The road contained two parallel indentations and was the rusty red color of abandoned iron. It seemed to originate in a faraway line of blue hills on his right, plunging straight across the plain to the heat-muddled horizon on his left. The road contained no occupant except himself, not even a dust cloud to mark some hidden passage.

McKie was almost glad to feel the sniggertrance grip him.

"This is Tuluk," his caller said. "I was told to contact you as soon as I had anything to report. Hopefully, I intrude at an opportune moment."

McKie, who had a journeyman's respect for Tuluk's competence, said, "Let's have it."

"Not much on the arm," Tuluk said. "Palenki, of course. We can identify the original owner, if we ever get him. There'd been at least one previous regrowth of this member. Sword cut on the forearm, by the look of it."

"What about the phylum markings?"

"We're still checking that."

"The whip?"

"That's something else. It's real steerhide."

"Real?"

59

"No doubt of it. We could identify the original owner of the skin, although I doubt it's walking around anywhere."

"You've a gruesome sense of humor. What else?"

"The whip's an archaism, too. Bullwhip, ancient earth style. We got an original ID by computer and brought in a museum expert for confirmation. He thought the construction was a bit on the crude side, but close enough to leave little doubt it was a copy of a real original. Fairly recent manufacture, too."

"Where could they get an original to copy?"

"We're checking that, and it may provide a lead. These things aren't too common."

"Recent manufacture," McKie said. "You sure?"

"The animal from which that hide was removed has been dead about two standard years. Intracellular structure was still reactive to catalyzing."

"Two years. Where would they get a real steer?"

"That narrows it down. There are some around for story props in the various entertainment media, that sort of thing. A few of the outback planets where they haven't the technology for pseudoflesh still raise cattle for food."

"This thing gets more confusing the deeper we go into it," McKie said.

"That's what we think. Oh, there's chalf dust on the whip."

"Chalf! That's where I got the yeast smell!"

"Yes, it's still quite strong."

"What would they be doing with that much quick-scribe powder?" McKie asked. "There was no sign of a chalf-memory stick—but that means little, of course."

"It's just a suggestion," Tuluk said, "but they couldn've chalf-scribed that design on the Palenki."

"Why?"

"Give it a false phylum, maybe?"

"Perhaps."

"If you smelled chalf after the whip came through, there'd have to be quite a bit of it around. You thought of that?"

"The room wasn't all that big, and it was hot."

"The heat would explain it, all right. Sorry we didn't have more for you."

"That's all?"

"Well, it might not be any use, but the whip had been stored in a hanging position supported by a thin length of steel."

"Steel? Are you positive?"

"Positive."

"Who still uses steel?"

"It's not all that uncommon on some of the newer planets. R&R has even turned up some where they build with it."

"Wild!"

"Isn't it, though?"

"You know," McKie said, "We're looking for an outback planet, and that's where I seem to be."

"Where are you?"

"I don't know."

"You don't know?"

McKie explained his predicament.

"You field agents take awful chances sometimes," Tuluk said.

"Don't we just."

"You wear a monitor. I could ask this Taprisiot to identify your location. Want to invoke the monitor clause?"

"You know that's an open payment clause," McKie said. "I don't think this is a sufficient emergency yet that I can risk bankrupting us. Let me see if I can identify this place by other means first."

"What do you want me to do, then?"

"Call Furuneo. Have him allow me another six hours, then get the Caleban to pick me up."

"Pick you up, right. Siker said you were onto some doorless S'eye thing. Can it pick you up anywhere?"

"I think so."

"I'll call Furuneo right away."

Facts can be whatever you want them to be. This is the lesson of relativity.

—BuSab Manual

McKie had been walking for almost two hours before he saw the smoke. Thin spirals of it stood in the air against the backdrop of distant blue hills.

It had occurred to McKie during his walk that he might have been set down in a place where he could die of thirst or starvation before his legs carried him to the safe companionship of his civilized fellows. A self-accusatory moroseness had overtaken him. It wasn't the first time he had realized that some accident of the machinery he took for granted might prove fatal.

But the *machinery* of his own mind? He cursed himself for using the Caleban's S'eye system this way when he knew the unreliability of communication with the creature.

Walking!

You never thought you might have to walk to safety.

McKie sensed the eternal flaw in sentient relationship with machinery. Reliance on such forces put your own muscles at a disadvantage in a universe where you might have to rely on those muscles at any moment.

Such as right now.

He appeared to be getting nearer to the smoke, although the hills looked as remote as ever.

Walking.

Of all the stupid damn foul-ups. Why would Abnethe pick a place like this to start her kinky little game? If this were the place it had started. If the Caleban hadn't made another communication error.

If love could find a way. What the devil did love have to do with all this?

McKie plodded on, wishing he had brought some water.

First the heat of the Beachball, now this. His throat felt as though he'd built a fire in it. The dust kicked up by his feet didn't help. Every step stirred up a puff of pale red from the narrow track. The dust clogged his throat and nostrils. It had a musty taste.

He patted the toolkit in his jacket pocket. The raygen could burn a thin hole in this parched earth, might even strike down to water. But how could he bring the water up to his demanding throat?

Plenty of insects around. They buzzed and flew about, crawled at the edge of the track, attempted at times to alight on his exposed flesh. He finally took to carrying his toolkit's stim like a fan, setting it at medium potency. It cleared the air around his face whenever a swarm approached, dropped jittering patches of stunned insects behind him.

He grew aware of a noise—low, indistinct booming. Something being pounded. Something hollow and resonant. It originated out there in the distance where the smoke stood on the air.

It could be a natural phenomenon, McKie told himself. Could be wild creatures. The smoke might be natural fires. Still, he brought the raygen from his kit, kept it in a side pocket where he could get at it quickly.

The noise became louder in slow stages, as though it were being amplified to mark consecutive positions of his approach. Screens of thornbush and gentle undulations in the plain concealed the source.

McKie trudged up a gentle rise, still following the road.

Sadness transfixed him. He'd been cast away on some poverty-stricken backyard world, a place that stiffened the eyes. He'd been given a role in a story with a moral, a clipped-wing fairy story. He was a burned-out wanderer, his thirst a burnished yearning. Anguish had lodged in him somewhere. He pursued an estranged, plodding dream which would dissolve in the awakening doom of a single Caleban.

The toll that Caleban's death would bring oppressed him. It turned his ego upside down and drained out all the lightness. His own death would be a lost bubble burst in such a conflagration.

McKie shook his head to drive away such thoughts. Fear

would pluck him of all sensibility. He could not afford it.

One thing sure now; the sun was setting. It had descended at least two widths toward the horizon since he'd started this stupid trek.

What in the name of the infinite devils was that drumming? It came at him as though riding the heat: monotonous, insistent. He felt his temples throbbing to an irritating counterpoint—beat, throb, beat, throb. . . .

McKie topped the low rise, stopped. He stood at the brim of a shallow basin which had been cleared of the thornbush. At the basin's center, a thorn fence enclosed twenty or so conical huts with grass roofs. They appeared to be made of mud. Smoke spiraled from holes in several of the roofs and from pit fires outside others. Black dots of cattle grazed in the basin, lifting their heads occasionally, with stubby whiskers of brown grass protruding from their mouths.

Black-skinned youths carrying long poles watched the cattle. More black-skinned men, women, and children went about various occupations within the thorn enclosure.

McKie, whose ancestry contained blacks from the planet Caoleh, found the scene curiously disturbing. It touched a genetic memory that vibrated to a wrong rhythm. Where in the universe could people be degraded to such primitive living standards? The basin was like a textbook scene from the dark ages of ancient Earth.

Most of the children were naked, as were some of the men. The women wore string skirts.

Could this be some odd return to nature? McKie wondered. The nudity didn't bother him particularly. It was the combination.

The narrow track led down into the basin and through the thorn fence, extending out the other side to disappear over the crest of the opposite side.

McKie began the descent. He hoped they'd let him have water in this village.

The booming noise came from within a large hut near the center of the cluster. A two-wheeled cart with four great two-horned beasts yoked to it waited beside the hut.

McKie studied the cart as he approached. Between its high sidewalls were piled jumbles of strange artifacts—flat, boardlike things, rolls of garish fabric, long poles with sharp metal tips.

The drumming stopped, and McKie noted that he had been seen. Children ran screaming among the huts, pointing at him. Adults turned with slow dignity, studied him.

An odd silence settled over the scene.

McKie entered the village through a break in the thorn fence. Emotionless black faces turned to observe his progress. The place assaulted McKie's nostrils—rotting flesh, dung, acrid stenches whose character he didn't care to explore, woodsmoke and burning meat.

Clouds of black insects swarmed about the beasts yoked to the cart, seeming to ignore the slow switching of their tails.

A red-bearded white man emerged from the larger hut as McKie approached. The man wore a flat-brimmed hat, dusty black jacket, and dun pants. He carried a whip of the same pattern the Palenki had used. Seeing the whip, McKie knew he had come to the right place.

The man waited in the doorway, a mean-eyed, menacing figure, thin lips visible through the beard. He glanced once at McKie, nodded at several of the black men off to McKie's left, motioned toward the cart, returned his attention to McKie.

Two tall black men moved to stand at the heads of the yoked beasts.

McKie studied the contents of the cart. The boardlike objects, he saw, had been carved and painted with strange designs. They reminded him of Palenki carapaces. He didn't like the way the two men at the heads of the yoked beasts stared at him. There was danger here. McKie kept his right hand in his jacket pocket, curled around the raygen tube. He felt and saw the black residents closing in behind him. His back felt exposed and vulnerable.

"I am Jorj X. McKie, Saboteur Extraordinary," he said, stopping about ten paces from the bearded white man. "And you?"

The man spat in the dust, said something that sounded like: "Getnabent."

McKie swallowed. He didn't recognize the greeting. Strange, he thought. He hadn't believed the ConSentiency

65

contained a language completely unfamiliar to him. Perhaps R&R had come up with a new planet here.

"I am on an official mission of the Bureau," McKie said. "Let all men know this." There, that satisfied the legalities.

The bearded man shrugged, said, "Kawderwelsh."

Someone behind McKie said: "Krawl'ikido!"

The bearded man glanced in the direction of the voice, back to McKie.

McKie shifted his attention to the whip. The man trailed the end of it behind him on the ground. Seeing McKie's attention, he flicked a wrist, caught the flexible end of the whip in two fingers which he lifted from the handle. He continued to stare at McKie.

There was a casual proficiency in the way the man handled the whip that sent a shudder through McKie. "Where'd you get that whip?" he asked.

The man looked at the object in his hand. "Pitsch," he said. "Brawzhenbuller."

McKie moved closer, held out a hand for the whip.

The bearded man shook his head from side to side, scowled. No mistaking that answer. "Maykely," he said. He tapped the butt of the whip handle against the side of the cart, nodded at the piled cargo.

Once more, McKie studied the contents of the cart. Handmade artifacts, no doubt of it. There could be a big profit in esoteric and decorative objects, he knew. These could be artifacts that curried to the buyer boredom brought on by the endless, practical, serial duplications from automatic factories. If they were manufactured in this village, though, the whole operation looked to be a slave-labor thing. Or serfdom, which was the same thing for all practical purposes.

Abnethe's *game* might have sicker overtones, but it had more understandable motives.

"Where's Mliss Abnethe?" he asked.

That brought a response. The bearded man jerked his head up, glared at McKie. The surrounding mob emitted an unintelligible cry.

"Abnethe?" McKie asked.

"Seeawss Abnethe!" the bearded man said.

The crowd around them began chanting: "Epah Abnethe! Epah Abnethe! Epah Abnethe!"

66

"Rooik!" the bearded man shouted.

The chant stopped abruptly.

"What is the name of this planet?" McKie asked. He glanced around at the staring black faces. "Where is this place?"

No one answered.

McKie locked eyes with the bearded man. The other returned his stare in a predatory, measuring manner, nodded once, as though he'd come to some conclusion. "Dees-pawng!" he said.

McKie frowned, swore under his breath. This damned case presented communication difficulties at every turn! No matter. He'd seen enough here to demand a full-scale investigation by a police agency. You didn't keep humans in this primitive state. Abnethe must be behind this place. The whip, the reaction to her name. The village smelled of Abnethe's sickness. McKie observed some of the people across from him, saw scars on their arms and chests. Whip scars? If they were, Abnethe's money wouldn't save her. She might get off with another reconditioning, but this time there'd be a more thorough . . .

Something exploded against the back of McKie's neck, knocking him forward. The bearded man raised the whip handle, and McKie saw the thing rushing toward his head. He felt a giant, coughing darkness lurch across his mind as the thing crashed against the side of his head. He tried to bring the raygen out of his pocket, but his muscles disobeyed. He felt his body become a limping, horrified stagger. His vision was a bloody haze.

Again something exploded against his head.

McKie sank into nightmare oblivion. As he sank, he thought of the monitor in his skull. If they had killed him, a Taprisiot somewhere would jerk to attention and send in a final report on one Jorj X. McKie.

A lot of good that'll do me! the darkness said.

Where is the weapon with which I enforce your bond-age? You give it to me every time you open your mouth.

—Laclac Riddle

There was a moon, McKie realized. That glowing thing directly in front of him had to be a moon. The realization told him he'd been seeing the moon for some time, puzzling over it without being fully awake. The moon had lifted itself out of blackness above a paralyzed outline of primitive roofs.

He was still in the village, then.

The moon dangled there, incredibly close.

The back and left side of McKie's head began throbbing painfully. He explored his bruised senses, realized he had been staked out in the open flat on his back, wrists and ankles tightly bound, his face pointed at the sky.

Perhaps it was another village.

He tested the security of his bindings, couldn't loosen them.

It was an undignified position: flat on his back, legs spread, arms outstretched.

For a time, he watched the changing guard of strange constellations move across his field of vision. Where was this place?

Firelight blazed up somewhere off to his left. It flickered, sank back to orange gloom. McKie tried to turn his head toward it, froze as pain stabbed upward from his neck through his skull.

He groaned.

Off in the darkness an animal screamed. The scream was followed by a hoarse, grunting roar. Silence. Then another roar. The sounds creased the night for McKie, bent it into new dimensions. He heard soft footsteps approaching.

"I think he groaned," a man said.

The man was speaking standard Galach, McKie noted. Two shadows came out of the night and stood over McKie's feet.

"Do you think he's awake?" It was a female voice masked by a *storter.*

"He's breathing as though he's awake," the man said.

"Who's there?" McKie rasped. His own voice sent agony pinwheeling through his skull.

"Good thing your people know how to obey instructions," the man said. "Imagine him running loose around here!"

"How did you get here, McKie?" the woman asked.

"I walked," McKie growled. "Is that you, Abnethe?"

"He walked!" the man snarled.

McKie, listening to that male voice, began to wonder about it. There was a trace of alien sibilance in it. Was it human or humanoid? Among the sentients only a Pan Spechi could look that human—because they had shaped their flesh to the human pattern.

"Unless you release me," McKie said, "I won't answer for the consequences."

"You'll answer for them," the man said. There was laughter in his voice.

"We must be sure how he got here," the woman said.

"What difference does it make?"

"It could make a great deal of difference. What if Fanny Mae is breaking her contract?"

"That's impossible!" the man snorted.

"Nothing's impossible. He couldn't have got here without Caleban help."

"Maybe there's another Caleban."

"Fanny Mae says not."

"I say we do away with this intruder immediately," the man said.

"What if he's wearing a monitor?" she asked.

"Fanny Mae says no Taprisiot can locate this place!"

"But McKie is here!"

"And I've had one long-distance call since I arrived," McKie said. *No Taprisiot can locate this place?* he wondered. What would prompt that statement?

"They won't have time to find us or do anything about it,"

69

the man said. "I say we do away with him."

"That wouldn't be very intelligent," McKie said.

"Look who's talking about intelligence," the man said.

McKie strained to discern details of faces, but they remained blank shadows. What was it about that male voice? The *storter* disguised the woman's voice, but why would she bother?

"I am fitted with a life monitor," McKie said.

"The sooner, the better," the man said.

"I've stood as much of that as I can," the woman said.

"Kill me, and that monitor starts transmitting," McKie said. "Taprisiots will scan this area and idenitfy everyone around me. Even if they can't locate you, they'll know you."

"I shudder at the prospect," the man said.

"We must find out how he got here," the woman said.

"What difference does it make?"

"That's a *stupid* question!"

"So the Caleban broke her contract."

"Or there's a loophole in it we don't know about."

"Well, plug it up."

"I don't know if we can. Sometimes I wonder how much we really understand each other. What are connectives?"

"Abnethe, why're you wearing that storter?" McKie asked.

"Why do you call me Abnethe?" she asked.

"You can disguise your voice, but you can't hide your sickness or your style," McKie said.

"Did Fanny Mae send you here?" she demanded.

"Didn't somebody say that was impossible?" McKie countered.

"He's a brave one," the woman chuckled.

"Lot of good it does him."

"I don't think the Caleban could break our contract," she said. "You recall the protection clause? It's likely she sent him here to get rid of him."

"So let's get rid of him."

"That's not what I meant!"

"You know we have to do it."

"You're making him suffer, and I won't have it!" the woman cried.

"Then go away and leave it to me."

"I can't stand the *thought* of him suffering! Don't you understand?"

"He won't suffer."

"You have to be sure."

It's Abnethe for certain, McKie thought, recalling her conditioning against witnessing pain. *But who's the other one?*

"My head's hurting," McKie said. "You know that, Mliss? Your men practically beat my brains out."

"What brains?" the man asked.

"We must get him to a doctor," she said.

"Be sensible!" the man snapped.

"You heard him. His head hurts."

"Mliss, stop it!"

"You used my name," she said.

"What difference does it make? He'd already recognized you."

"What if he escapes?"

"From here?"

"He got here, didn't he?"

"For which we can be thankful!"

"He's suffering," she said.

"He's lying!"

"He's suffering. I can tell."

"What if we take him to a doctor, Mliss?" the man asked, "What if we do that and he escapes? BuSab agents are resourceful, you know."

Silence.

"There's no way out of it," the man said. "Fanny Mae sent him to us, and we have to kill him."

"You're trying to drive me crazy!" she screamed.

"He won't suffer," the man said.

Silence.

"I promise," the man said.

"For sure?"

"Didn't I say it?"

"I'm leaving here," she said. "I don't want to know what happens to him. You're never to mention him again, Cheo. Do you hear me?"

71

"Yes, my dear, I hear you."

"I'm leaving now," she said.

"He's going to cut me into little pieces," McKie said, "and I'll scream with pain the whole time."

"Shut him up!" she screeched.

"Come away, my dear," the man said. He put an arm around her. "Come along, now."

Desperately, McKie said, "Abnethe! He's going to cause me intense pain. You *know* that."

She began sobbing as the man led her away. "Please . . . please . . ." she begged. The sound of her crying faded into the night.

Furuneo, McKie thought, *don't dally. Get that Caleban moving. I want out of here. Now!*

He strained against his bindings. They stretched just enough to tell him he'd reached their limits. He couldn't feel the stakes move at all.

Come on, Caleban! McKie thought. *You didn't send me here to die. You said you loved me.*

*It is because you speak to me that I do not believe in
you.*

—Quoted from a Caleban

After several hours of questioning, counter-questioning,
probe, counter-probe, and bootless answers, Furuneo
brought in an enforcer assistant to take over the watch on the
Caleban. At Furuneo's request Fanny Mae opened a portal
and let him out onto the lava ledge for a spell of fresh air. It
was cold out on the shelf, especially after the heat in the
Beachball. The wind had died down, as it did most days here
just before night. Surf still pounded the outer rocks and
surged against the lava wall beyond the Beachball. But the
tide was going out, and only a few dollops of spray wet the
ledge.

Connectives, Furuneo thought bitterly. *She says it's not a
linkage, so what is it?* He couldn't recall ever having felt this
frustrated.

"That which extends from one to eight," the Caleban had
said, "that is a connective. Correct use of verb to be?"

"Huh?"

"Identity verb," the Caleban said. "Strange concept."

"No, no! What did you mean there, one to eight?"

"Unbinding stuff," the Caleban said.

"You mean like a solvent?"

"Before solvent."

"What the devil could *before* have to do with solvents?"

"Perhaps more internal than solvents," the Caleban said.

"Madness," Furuneo said, shaking his head. Then,
"Internal?"

"Unbounded place of connectives," the Caleban said.

"We're right back where we started," Furuneo groaned.
"What's a connective?"

"Uncontained opening between," the Caleban said.

73

"Between *what?*" Furuneo roared.

"Between one and eight."

"Ohhh, no!"

"Also between one and *x,*" the Caleban said.

As McKie had done earlier, Furuneo buried his face in his hands. Presently he said, "What's between one and eight except two, three, four, five, six, and seven?"

"Infinity," the Caleban said. "Open-ended concept. Nothing contains everything. Everything contains nothing."

"You know what I think?" Furuneo asked.

"I read no thoughts," the Caleban said.

"I think you're having your little game with us," Furuneo said. "That's what I think."

"Connectives compel," the Caleban said. "Does this expand understanding?"

"Compels . . . a compulsion?"

"Venture movement," the Caleban said.

"Venture what?"

"That which remains stationary when all else moves," the Caleban said. "Thus, connective. Infinity concept empties itself without connective."

"Whooooooheee!" Furuneo said.

At this point he asked to be let outside for a rest.

Furuneo was no closer to understanding why the Caleban maintained such a high temperature in the Beachball.

"Consequences of swiftness," the Caleban said, varying this under questioning with "Rapidity convergence." Or "Perhaps concept of generated movement arrives closer."

"Some kind of friction?" Furuneo probed.

"Uncompensated relationship of dimensions possibly arrives at closest approximation," the Caleban answered.

Now, reviewing these frustrating exchanges, Furuneo blew on his hands to warm them. The sun had set, and a chill wind was beginning to move off the bluff toward the water.

Either I freeze to death or bake, he thought. *Where in the universe is McKie?*

At this point Tuluk made long distance contact through one of the Bureau Taprisiots. Furuneo, who had been seeking a more sheltered position in the lee of the Beachball, felt the pineal ignition. He brought down the foot he had been lifting in a step, planted the foot firmly in a shallow pool of water, and lost all bodily sensation. Mind and call were one.

"This is Tuluk at the lab," the caller said. "Apologies for intrusion and all that."

"I think you just made me put a foot in cold water," Furuneo said.

"Well, here's some more cold water for you. You're to have that friendly Caleban pick up McKie in six hours, time elapse measured from four hours and fifty-one minutes ago. Synchronize."

"Standard measure?"

"Of course, standard!"

"Where is he?"

"He doesn't know. Wherever that Caleban sent him. Any idea how it's done?"

"It's done with connectives," Furuneo said.

"Is that right? What are connectives?"

"When I find out, you'll be the first to know."

"That sounds like a temporal contradiction, Furuneo."

"Probably is. All right, let me get my foot out of the water. It's probably frozen solid by now."

"You've the synchronized time coordinate for picking up McKie?"

"I got it! And I hope she doesn't send him home."

"How's that?"

Furuneo explained.

"Sounds confusing."

"I'm glad you figured that out. For a moment there, I thought you weren't approaching our problem with sufficient seriousness."

Among Wreaves seriousness and sincerity are almost as basic as they are with Taprisiots, but Tuluk had worked among humans long enough to recognize the jibe. "Well, every being has its own insanity," he said.

It was a Wreave aphorism, but it sounded sufficiently close to something the Caleban might have said that Furuneo experienced a momentary *angeret*-enforced rage and sensed his ego shimmering away from him. He shuddered his way back to mental solidity.

"Did you almost lose yourself?" Tuluk asked.

"Will you sign off and let me get my foot out of the water?"

"I receive the impression you are fatigued," Tuluk said. "Get some rest."

"When I can. I hope I don't fall asleep in the Caleban hothouse. I'd wake up done just about right for a cannibal dinner."

"Sometimes you humans express yourselves in a disgusting fashion," the Wreave said. "But you'd better remain alert for a while. McKie may require punctuality."

He was the kind of man who created his own death.

—Epitaph for Alichino Furuneo

It was dark, but she needed no light for black thoughts.

Damn Cheo for a sadistic fool! It had been a mistake to finance the surgery that had transformed the Pan Spechi into an ego-frozen freak. Why couldn't he stay the way he'd been when they'd first met? So exotic . . . so . . . so . . . exciting.

He was still useful, though. And there was no doubt he'd been the first to see the magnificent possibilities in their discovery. That, at least, remained exciting.

She reclined on a softly furred chairdog, one of the rare feline adaptives that had been taught to lull their masters by purring. The soothing vibrations moved through her flesh as though seeking out irritations to subdue. So relaxing.

She sighed.

Her apartment occupied the top ring of the tower they had had built on this world, safe in the knowledge that their hiding place lay beyond the reach of any law or any communication except that granted through a single Caleban—who had but a short time to live.

But how had McKie come here? And what had McKie meant, that he'd had a call through a Taprisiot?

The chairdog, sensitive to her mood, stopped purring as Abnethe sat up. Had Fanny Mae lied? Did another Caleban remain who could find this place?

Granted that the Caleban's words were difficult to understand—granted this, yes, there was yet no mistaking the essentials. This world was a place whose key lay in only one mind, that of Madame Mliss Abnethe.

She sat straight on the chairdog.

And there would be death without suffering to make this place forever safe—a giant orgasm of death. Only one door,

77

and death would close it. The survivors, all chosen by herself, would live on in happiness here beyond all . . . connectives . . .

Whatever those were.

She stood up, began pacing back and forth in the darkness. The rug, a creature adapted like the chairdog, squirmed its furry surface at the caress of her feet.

An amused smile came over her face.

Despite the complications and the strange timing it required, they'd have to increase the tempo of the floggings. Fanny Mae must be forced to discontinue as soon as possible. To kill without suffering among the victims, this was a prospect she found she could still contemplate.

But there was need for hurry.

Furuneo leaned, half dozing, against a wall within the Beachball. Sleepily he cursed the heat. His mindclock said there was slightly less than an hour remaining until the time for picking up McKie. Furuneo had tried to explain the time schedule to the Caleban, but she persisted in misunderstanding.

"Lengths extend and distend," she had said. "They warp and sift with vague movements between one and another. Thus time remains inconstant."

Inconstant?

The vortal tube of a S'eye jumpdoor snapped open just beyond the Caleban's giant spoon. The face and bare shoulders of Abnethe appeared in the opening.

Furuneo pushed himself away from the wall, shook his head to restore alertness. Damnation, it was hot in here!

"You are Alichino Furuneo," Abnethe said. "Do you know me?"

"I know you."

"I recognized you at once," she said. "I know most of your stupid Bureau's planetary agents by sight. I've found it profitable."

"Are you here to flog this poor Caleban?" Furuneo asked. He felt for the holoscan in his pocket, moved into a position for a rush toward the jumpdoor as McKie had ordered.

"Don't make me close this door before we've had a little discussion," she said.

Furuneo hesitated. He was no Saboteur Extraordinary, but you didn't get to be a planetary agent without recognizing when to disobey a senior agent's orders.

"What's to discuss?" he asked.

"Your future," she said.

Furuneo stared up into her eyes. The emptiness of them appalled him. This woman was ridden by a compulsion.

"My future?" he asked.

"Whether you're to have *any* future," she said.

"Don't threaten me," he said.

"Cheo tells me," she said, "that you're a possibility for our project."

For no reason he could explain, Furuneo knew this to be a lie. Odd how she gave herself away. Her lips trembled when she said that name—Cheo.

"Who's Cheo?" he asked.

"That's unimportant at the moment."

"What's your project, then?"

"Survival."

"That's nice," he said. "What else is new?" He wondered what she would do if he brought out the holoscan and started recording.

"Did Fanny Mae send McKie hunting for me?" she asked.

That question was important to her, Furuneo saw. McKie must have stirred up merry hob.

"You've seen McKie?" he asked.

"I refuse to discuss McKie," she said.

It was an insane response, Furuneo thought. She'd been the one to bring McKie into the conversation.

Abenthe pursed her lips, studied him. "Are you married, Alichino Furuneo?" she asked.

He frowned. Her lips had trembled again. Surely she knew his marital status. If it was valuable for her to recognize him, it was thrice valuable to know his strengths and weaknesses. What was her game?

"My wife is dead," he said.

"How sad," she murmured.

"I get along," he said, angry. "You can't live in the past."

79

"Ahhh, that is where you may be wrong," she said.

"What're you driving at, Abnethe?"

"Let's see," she said, "your age—sixty-seven standard, if I recall correctly."

"You recall correctly, as you damn well know."

"You're young," she said. "You look even younger. I'd guess you're a vital person who enjoys life."

"Don't we all?" he asked.

It was going to be a bribe offer, then, he thought.

"We enjoy life when we have the proper ingredients," she said. "How odd it is to find a person such as yourself in that stupid Bureau."

This was close enough to a thought Furuneo had occasionally nurtured for himself that he began wondering about this Cheo and the mysterious project with its possibilities. What were they offering?

They studied each other for a moment. It was the weighted assessment of two contestants about to enter a competition.

Would she offer herself? Furuneo wondered. She was an attractive female: generous mouth, large green eyes, a pleasant oval face. He'd seen the holoscans of her figure—the Beautybarbers had done well by her. She'd maintained herself with all the expensive care her money could buy. But would she offer herself to him? He found this difficult to contemplate. Motives and stakes didn't fit.

"What're you afraid of?" he asked.

It was a good opening attack, but she answered him with a peculiar note of sincerity: "Suffering."

Furuneo tried to swallow in a dry throat. He hadn't been celibate since Mada's death, but that had been a special kind of marriage. It had gone beyond words and bodies. If anything remained solid and basic, *connective,* in the universe, their kind of love did. He had but to close his eyes to feel the memory-presence of her. Nothing could replace that, and Abnethe must know it. She couldn't offer him anything unobtainable elsewhere.

Or could she?

"Fanny Mae," Abnethe said, "are you prepared to honor the request I made?"

"Connective appropriate," the Caleban said.

"Connectives!" Furuneo exploded. "What are connectives?"

"I don't really know," Abnethe said, "but apparently I can exploit them without knowing."

"What're you cooking up?" Furuneo demanded. He wondered why his skin felt suddenly chilled in spite of the heat.

"Fanny Mae, show him," Abnethe said.

The jumpdoor's vortal tube flickered open, closed, danced and shimmered. Abruptly, Abnethe no longer was visible in it. The door stood open once more, looking down now onto a sunny jungle shore, a softly heaving ocean surface, an oval stabo-yacht hanging in stasis above a clearing and a sandy beach. The yacht's afterdeck shields lay open to the sun, exposing almost in the center of the deck a young woman stretched out in repose, facedown on a floater hammock. Her body was drinking the rays of a tuned sun filter.

Furuneo stared, unable to move. The young woman lifted her head, stared out to sea, lay back.

Abnethe's voice came from directly over his head, another jumpdoor obviously, but he couldn't take his gaze from that well-remembered scene. "You recognize this?" she asked.

"It's Mada," he whispered.

"Precisely."

"Oh, my god," he whispered. "When did you scan that?"

"It is your beloved, you're sure?" Abnethe asked.

"It's . . . it's our honeymoon," he whispered. "I even know the day. Friends took me to visit the seadome, but she didn't enjoy swimming and stayed behind."

"How do you know the actual day?"

"The flambok tree at the edge of the clearing: It bloomed that day, and I missed it. See the umbrella flower?"

"Oh, yes. Then you've no doubt about the authenticity of this scene?"

"So you had your snoopers staring at us even then?" he rasped.

"Not snoopers. We are the snoopers. This is now."

"It can't be! That was almost forty years ago!"

"Keep your voice down, or she'll hear you."

"How can she hear me? She's been dead for . . ."

"This is now, I tell you! Fanny Mae?"

"In person of Furuneo, concept of now contains relative connectives," the Caleban said. "Nowness of scene true."

Furuneo shook his head from side to side.

"We can pluck her from that yacht and take both of you to a place the Bureau will never find," Abnethe said. "What do you think of that, Furuneo?"

Furuneo wiped tears from his cheeks. He was aware of the sea's ozone smell, the pungency of the flambok blossom. It had to be a recording, though. Had to be.

"If it's now, why hasn't she seen us?" he asked.

"At my direction Fanny Mae masks us from her sight. Sound, however, will carry. Keep your voice down."

"You're lying!" he hissed.

As though at a signal, the young woman rolled over, stood up, and admired the flambok. She began humming a song familiar to Furuneo.

"I think you know I'm not lying," Abnethe said. "This is our secret, Furuneo. This is our discovery about the Calebans."

"But . . . how can . . ."

"Given the proper connectives, whatever they are, even the past is open to us. Only Fanny Mae of all the Calebans remains to link us with this past. No Taprisiot, no Bureau, nothing can reach us there. We can go there and free ourselves forever."

"This is a trick!" he said.

"You can see it isn't. Smell that flower, the sea."

"But why . . . what do you want?"

"Your assistance in a small matter, Furuneo."

"How?"

"We fear someone will stumble on our secret before we're ready. If, however, someone the Bureau trusts is here to watch and report—giving a false report . . ."

"What false report?"

"That there've been no more floggings, that Fanny Mae is happy, that . . ."

"Why should I do that?"

"When Fanny Mae reaches her . . . ultimate discontinuity, we can be far away and safe—you with your beloved. Correct, Fanny Mae?"

82

"Truthful essence in statement," the Caleban said.

Furuneo stared through the jumpdoor. Mada! She was right there. She had stopped humming and was coating her body with a skin-protective. If the Caleban moved the door a little closer, he knew he'd be able to reach out and touch his beloved.

Pain in Furuneo's chest made him aware of a constriction there. The past!

"Am . . . I down there somewhere?" he asked.

"Yes," Abnethe said.

"And I'll come back to the yacht?"

"If that's what you did originally."

"What would I find, though?"

"Your bride gone, disappeared."

"But . . ."

'It would be thought that some creature of the sea or the jungle killed her. Perhaps she went swimming and . . ."

"She lived thirty-one years after that," he whispered.

"And you can have those thirty-one years all over again," Abnethe said.

"I . . . I wouldn't be the same. She'd . . ."

"She'd know you."

Would she really? he wondered. Perhaps—yes. Yes, she'd know him. She might even come to understand the need behind such a decision. But he saw quite clearly that she'd never forgive him. Not Mada.

"With proper care she might not have to die in thirty-one years," Abnethe said.

Furuneo nodded, but it was a gesture only for himself.

She wouldn't forgive him any more than the young man returning to an empty yacht could forgive him. And that young man had not died.

I couldn't forgive myself, he thought. *The young man I was would never forgive me all those lovely lost years.*

"If you're worried," Abnethe said, "about changing the universe or the course of history or any such nonsense, forget it. That's not how it works, Fanny Mae tells me. You change a single, isolated situation, no more. The new situation goes off about its business, and everything else remains pretty much the same."

"I see."

"Do you agree to our bargain?" Abnethe asked.

"What?"

"Shall I have Fanny Mae pick her up for you?"

"Why bother?" he asked. "I can't agree to such a thing."

"You're joking!"

He turned, stared up at her, saw that she had a small jumpdoor open almost directly over his head. Only her eyes, nose, and mouth could be seen through the opening.

"I am not joking."

Part of her hand became visible as she lifted it, pointed toward the other door. "Look down there at what you're rejecting. Look, I say! Can you honestly tell me you don't want that back?"

He turned.

Mada had gone back to the hammock, snuggled face-down against a pillow. Furuneo recalled that he'd found her like that when he'd returned from the seadome.

"You're not offering me anything," he said.

"But I am! It's true, everything I've told you!"

"You're a fool," he said, "if you can't see the difference between what Mada and I had and what you offer. I pity . . ."

Something fiercely compressive gripped his throat, choked off his words. Furuneo's hands groped in empty air as he was lifted up . . . up . . . He felt his head go through jumpdoor resistance. His neck was precisely within the boundary juncture when the door was closed. His body fell back into the Beachball.

Body jargon and hormone squirts, these begin to get at communication.

**Culture Lag, an unpublished work
by Jorj X. McKie**

"You fool, Mliss!" Cheo raged. "You utter, complete, senseless fool! If I hadn't come back when I . . ."

"You killed him!" she rasped, backing away from the bloody head on the floor of her sitting room. "You . . . you killed him! And just when I'd almost . . ."

"When you'd almost ruined everything," Cheo snarled, thrusting his scarred face close to her. "What do you humans use for brains?"

"But he'd . . ."

"He was ready to call his helpers and tell them everything you'd blurted to him!"

"I won't have you talking to me this way!"

"When it's my neck you're putting on the block, I'll talk to you any way I want."

"You made him suffer!" she accused.

"He didn't feel a thing from what I did. You're the one who made him suffer."

"How can you say that?" She backed away from the Pan Spechi face with its frighteningly oversized humanoid features.

"You bleat about being unable to stand suffering," he growled, "but you *love* it. You cause it all around you! You *knew* Furuneo wouldn't accept your stupid offer, but you taunted him with it, with what he'd lost. You don't call *that* suffering?"

"See here, Cheo, if you . . ."

"He suffered right up to the instant I put a stop to it," the Pan Spechi said. "And you *know* it!"

"Stop it!" she screamed. "I didn't! He wasn't!"

85

"He was and you knew it, every instant of it, you knew it."

She rushed at him, beat her fists against his chest. "You're lying! You're lying! You're lying!"

He grabbed her wrists, forced her to her knees. She lowered her head. Tears ran down her cheeks. "Lies, lies, lies," she muttered.

In a softer, more reasonable tone, he said: "Mliss, hear me. We've no way to know how much longer the Caleban can last. Be sensible. We've a limited number of fixed periods when we can use the S'eye, and we have to make the most of them. You've wasted one of those periods. We can't afford such blunders, Mliss."

She kept her gaze down, refused to look at him.

"You know I don't like to be severe with you, Mliss," he said, "but my way is best—as you've said yourself many times. We've our own ego-integrity to preserve."

She nodded without looking at him.

"Let's join the others now," he said. "Plouty has devised an amusing new game."

"One thing," she said.

"Yes?"

"Let's save McKie. He'd be an interesting addition to . . ."

"No."

"What harm could it do? He might even be useful. It isn't as though he'd have his precious Bureau or anything to enforce his . . ."

"No! Besides, it's probably too late. I've already sent the Palenki with . . . well, you understand."

He released her wrists.

Abnethe got to her feet, nostrils flaring. She looked up at him then, eyes peering through her lashes, her head tilted forward. Suddenly her right foot lashed out, caught Cheo with a hard heel in the left shin.

He danced back, nursed the bruise with one hand. Despite the pain, he was amused. "You see?" he said. "You *do* like suffering."

She was all over him then, kissing him, apologizing. They never did get down to Plouty's new game.

You can say things which cannot be done. This is elementary. The trick is to keep attention focused on what is said and not on what can be done.

—**BuSab Manual**

As Furuneo's life monitor ignited at his death, Taprisiots scanned the Beachball area. They found only the Caleban and four enforcers in hovering guard ships. Reasoning about actions, motives or guilt did not come within the Taprisiot scope. They merely reported the death, its location, and the sentients available to their scanners.

The four enforcers came in for several days of rough questioning as a result. The Caleban was a different matter. A full BuSab management conference was required before they could decide what action to take about the Caleban. Furuneo's death had come under extremely mysterious circumstances—no head, unintelligible responses from the Caleban.

As Tuluk entered the conference room on a summons that had roused him from sleep, Siker was flailing the table. He was using his middle fighting tendril for the gesture, quite un-Laclac in emotional intensity.

"We don't act without calling McKie!" Siker said. "This is too delicate!"

Tuluk took his position at the table, leaned into the Wreave support provided for his species, spoke mildly: "Haven't you contacted McKie yet? Furuneo was supposed to have ordered the Caleban . . ."

That was as far as he got. Explanations and data came at him from several of the others.

Presently Tuluk said, "Where's Furuneo's body?"

"Enforcers are bringing it to the lab now."

"Have the police been brought in?"

"Of course."

"Anything on the missing head?"

"No sign of it."

"Has to be the result of a jumpdoor," Tuluk said. "Will the police take over?"

"We're not going to allow that. One of our own."

Tuluk nodded. "I'm with Siker, then. We don't move without consulting McKie. This case was handed to him when we didn't know its extent. He's still in charge."

"Should we reconsider that decision?" someone down the table asked.

Tuluk shook his head. "Bad form," he said. "First things first. Furuneo's dead, and he was supposed to have ordered McKie's return some time ago."

Bildoon, the Pan Spechi chief of the Bureau, had watched this exchange with attentive silence. He had been ego holder of his pentarchal life group for seventeen years—a reasonably average time in his species. Although the thought revolted him in a way other species could never really understand, he knew he'd have to give up the ego to the youngest member of his crèche circle soon. The ego exchange would come sooner than it might have without the strains of command. Terrible price to pay in the service of sentience, he thought.

The humanoid appearance which his kind had genetically shaped and adopted had a tendency to beguile other humanoids into forgetting the essentially alien character of the Pan Spechi. The time would come, though, when they would be unable to avoid that awareness in Bildoon's case. His friends in the ConSentiency would see the crèche-change at its beginning—the glazing of the eyes, the rictus of the mouth. . . .

Best not think about that, he warned himself. He needed all his abilities right now.

He felt he no longer lived in his ego-self, and this was a sensation of exquisite torture for a Pan Spechi. But the black negation of all sentient life that threatened his universe demanded the sacrifice of personal fears. The Caleban must not be allowed to die. Until he had assured himself of the Caleban's survival, he must cling to any rope which life offered him, endure any terror, refuse to mourn for the almost-death-of-self that lurked in Pan Spechi nightmares. A greater death pressed upon them all.

Siker, he saw, was staring at him with an unspoken question.

Bildoon spoke three words: "Get a Taprisiot."

Someone near the door hurried to obey.

"Who was most recently in contact with McKie?" Bildoon asked.

"I believe I was," Tuluk said.

"It'll be easier for you, then," Bildoon said. "Make it short."

Tuluk wrinkled his facial slit in agreement.

A Taprisiot was led in, was helped up onto the table. It complained that they were being much too rough with its speech needles, that the embedment was imperfect, that they hadn't given it sufficient time to prepare its energies.

Only after Bildoon invoked the emergency clause of the Bureau's special contract would it agree to act. It positioned itself in front of Tuluk then, said, "Date, time, and place."

Tuluk gave the local coordinates.

"Close face," the Taprisiot ordered.

Tuluk obeyed.

"Think of contact," the Taprisiot squeaked.

Tuluk thought of McKie.

Time passed without contact. Tuluk opened his face, stared out.

"Close face!" the Taprisiot ordered.

Tuluk obeyed.

Bildoon said, "Is something wrong?"

"Hold silence," the Taprisiot said. "Disturb embedment." Its speech needles rustled. "Putcha, putcha," it said. "Call go when Caleban permit."

"Contact through a Caleban?" Bildoon ventured.

"Otherwise not available," the Taprisiot said. "McKie isolated in connectives of another being."

"I don't care how you get him, just get him!" Bildoon ordered.

Abruptly, Tuluk jerked as the sniggertrance marked pineal ignition.

"McKie?" he said. "Tuluk here."

The words, uttered through the mumbling of the snigger-trance, were barely audible to the others around the table.

Speaking as calmly as he could, McKie said, "McKie will

89

not be here in about thirty seconds unless you call Furuneo and have him order that Caleban to get me out of here.''

"What's wrong?" Tuluk asked.

"I'm staked out, and a Palenki is on its way to kill me. I can see it against the firelight. It's carrying what appears to be an ax. It's going to chop me up. You know how they . . ."

"I can't call Furuneo. He's . . ."

"Then call the Caleban!"

"You know you can't call a Caleban!"

"Do it, you oaf!"

Because McKie had ordered it, suspecting that he might know such a call would be made, Tuluk broke the contact, sent a demand at the Taprisiot. It was against reason: All the data said Taprisiots couldn't link sentients and Calebans.

To the observers in the conference room, the more obvious mumbling and chuckling of the sniggertrance faded, made a brief return, disappeared. Bildoon almost barked a question at Tuluk, hesitated. The Wreave's tubular body remained so . . . still.

"I wonder why the Tappy said he had to call through a Caleban," Siker whispered.

Bildoon shook his head.

A Chither near Tuluk said, "You know, I could swear he ordered the Taprisiot to *call* the Caleban."

"Nonsense," Siker said.

"I don't understand it," the Chither said. "How could McKie go somewhere and not know where he is?"

"Is Tuluk out of the sniggertrance or isn't he?" Siker asked, his voice fearful. "He acts like nobody's there."

Every sentient around the table froze into silence. They all knew what Siker meant. Had the Wreave been trapped in the call? Was Tuluk gone, taken into that strange limbo from which the personality never returned?

"NOW!" someone roared.

The assembled sentients jerked back from the conference table as McKie came tumbling out of nowhere in a shower of dust and dirt. He landed flat on his back on the table directly in front of Bildoon, who lifted half out of his chair. McKie's wrists were bloody, his eyes glazed, red hair tangled in a wild mop.

"Now," McKie whispered. He turned onto his side, saw Bildoon, and as though it explained everything, added, "The ax was descending."

"What ax?" Bildoon demanded, sliding back into his chair.

"The one the Palenki was aiming at my head."

"The . . . WHAT?"

McKie sat up, massaged his torn wrists where the bindings had held him. Presently he shifted his ministrations to his ankles. He looked like a Gowachin frog deity.

"McKie, explain what's going on here," Bildoon ordered.

"I . . . ahh, well, the nick of time was almost a fatal nick too late," McKie said. "What made Furuneo wait so long? He was told six hours, no more. Wasn't he?" McKie looked at Tuluk, who remained silent, stiff as a length of gray pipe against the Wreave support.

"Furuneo's dead," Bildoon said.

"Ahhh, damn," McKie said softly. "How?"

Bildoon made the explanation brief, then asked, "Where've you been? What's this about a Palenki with an ax?"

McKie, still sitting on the table, gave a neatly abbreviated chronological report. It sounded as though he were talking about a third person. He wound it up with a flat statement; "I have no idea at all where I was."

"They were going to . . . chop you up?" Bildoon asked.

"The ax was coming down," McKie said. "It was right there." He held up a hand about six centimeters from his nose.

Siker cleared his throat, said, "Something's wrong with Tuluk."

They all turned.

Tuluk remained propped against the support, his face slit closed. His body was there, but he wasn't.

"Is he . . . lost?" Bildoon rasped and turned away. If Tuluk failed to *come back* . . . how like the Pan Spechi ego-loss that would be!

"Somebody down there shake up that Taprisiot," McKie ordered.

"Why bother?" That was a human male from the Legal Department. "They never answer a question about . . . you know." He glanced uneasily at Bildoon, who remained with face averted.

"Tuluk made contact with the Caleban," McKie said, remembering. "I told him . . . it's the only way he could've done it with Furuneo dead." He stood up on the table, walked down its length to stand towering over the Taprisiot!

"You!" he shouted. "Taprisiot!"

Silence.

McKie drew a finger along an arm of speech needles. They clattered like a line of wooden clackers, but no intelligible sound came from the Taprisiot.

"You're not supposed to touch them," someone said.

"Get another Taprisiot in here," McKie ordered.

Someone ran to obey.

McKie mopped his forehead. It required all his reserves to keep from trembling. During the descent of the Palenki ax he had said goodbye to the universe. It had been final, irrevocable. He still felt that he had not returned, that he was watching the antics of some other creature in his own flesh, a familiar creature but a stranger, really. This room, the words and actions around him, were some sort of distorted play refined to blind sterility. In the instant when he had accepted his own death, he had realized there still remained uncounted things he wanted to experience. This room and his duties as a BuSab agent were not among those desires. The odd reality was drowned in selfish memories. Still, this flesh went through the motions. That was what training did.

A second Taprisiot was herded into the room, its needles squeaking complaints. It was hoisted onto the table, objecting all the way. "You *have* Taprisiot! Why you disturb?"

Bildoon turned back to the table, studied the scene, but remained silent, withdrawn. No one had ever been brought back from the long-distance trap.

McKie faced the new Taprisiot. "Can you contact this other Taprisiot?" he demanded.

"Putcha, putcha . . ." the second Taprisiot began.

"I'm sincere!" McKie blared.

"Ahseeda day-day," the second Taprisiot squeaked.

"I'll stack you with somebody's firewood if you don't get cracking," McKie snarled. "Can you make contact?"

"Who you call?" the second Taprisiot asked.

"Not me, you fugitive from a sawmill!" McKie roared. "Them!" He pointed at Tuluk and the first Taprisiot.

"They stuck to Caleban," the second Taprisiot said. "Who you call?"

"What do you mean, *stuck?*" McKie demanded.

"Tangled?" the Taprisiot ventured.

"Can either of them be called?" McKie asked.

"Untangle soon, then call," the Taprisiot said.

"Look!" Siker said.

McKie whirled.

Tuluk was flexing his facial slit. A mandibular extensor came out, withdrew.

McKie held his breath.

Tuluk's facial slit opened wide, and he said, "Fascinating."

"Tuluk?" McKie said.

The slit widened. Wreave eyes stared out. "Yes?" Then, "Ah, McKie. You made it."

"You call now?" the second Taprisiot asked.

"Get rid of him," McKie ordered.

Squeaking protests—"If you not call, why disturb?"— the Taprisiot was removed from the room.

"What happened to you, Tuluk?" McKie asked.

"Difficult to explain," the Wreave said.

"Try."

"Embedment," Tuluk said. "That has something to do with planetary conjunctions, whether the points linked by a call are aligned with each other across open space. There was some problem with this call, discontinuous through a stellar mass, perhaps, And it was contact with a Caleban . . . I don't appear to have the proper words."

"Do *you* understand what happened to you?"

"I think so. You know, I hadn't realized where I lived."

McKie stared at him, puzzled. "What?"

"Something's wrong here," Tuluk said. "Oh, yes: Furuneo."

"You said something about where you lived," McKie prodded.

"Space occupancy, yes," Tuluk said. "I live in a place with many . . . ahh, synonymous? yes, synonymous occupants."

"What're you talking about?" McKie asked.

"I was actually in contact with the Caleban during my call to you," Tuluk said. "Very odd, McKie. It was as though my call went through a pinhole in a black curtain, and the pinhole was the Caleban."

"So you contacted the Caleban," McKie prompted.

"Oh, yes. Indeed I did." Tuluk's mandibular extensors moved in a pattern indicative of emotional disturbance. "I saw! That's it. I saw . . . ahhh, many frames of parallel films. Of course, I didn't really *see* them. It was the eye."

"Eye? Whose eye?"

"That's the pinhole," Tuluk explained. "It's our eye, too, naturally."

"Do you understand any of this, McKie?" Bildoon asked.

"My impression is he's talking like a Caleban," McKie said. He shrugged. "Contaminated, perhaps. Entangled?"

"I suspect," Bildoon said, "that Caleban *communication* can be understood only by the certifiably insane."

McKie wiped perspiration from his lip. He felt he could *almost* understand what Tuluk had said. Meaning hovered right at the edge of awareness.

"Tuluk," Bildoon said, "try to tell us what happened to you. We don't understand you."

"I am trying."

"Keep at it," McKie said.

"You contacted the Caleban," Bildoon said. "How was that done? We've been told it's impossible."

"It was partly because the Caleban seemed to be handling my call to McKie," Tuluk said. "Then . . . McKie ordered me to call the Caleban. Perhaps it heard."

Tuluk closed his eyes, appeared lost in reverie.

"Go on," Bildoon said.

"I . . . it was. . . ." Tuluk shook his head, opened his eyes, stared pleadingly around the room. He met curious, probing eyes on all sides. "Imagine two spider-webs," he said. "Natural spiderwebs, now, not the kind they spin at our command . . . random products. Imagine that they must . . . contact each other . . . a certain congruity between them, an occlusion.''

"Like a *dental* occlusion?" McKie asked.

"Perhaps. At any rate, this necessary congruity, this *shape* required for contact, presumes proper connectives.''

McKie expelled a harsh breath. "What the devil are connectives?''

"I go now?" the first Taprisiot interrupted.

"Damn!" McKie said. "Somebody get rid of this thing!''

The Taprisiot was hustled from the room.

"Tuluk, what are connectives?" McKie demanded.

"Is this important?" Bildoon asked.

"Will you all take my word for it and let him answer?" McKie asked. "It's important. Tuluk?''

"Mmmmmm," Tuluk said. "You realize, of course, that artificiality can be refined to the point where it's virtually indistinguishable from original reality?''

"What's that have to do with connectives?''

"It's precisely at that point where the single distinguishing characteristic between original and artificial is the connective," Tuluk explained.

"Huh?" McKie said.

"Look at me," Tuluk said.

"I *am* looking at you!''

"Imagine that you take a food vat and produce in it an exact fleshly duplicate of my person," Tuluk said.

"An exact fleshly . . .''

"You could do it, couldn't you?" Tuluk demanded.

"Of course. But why?''

"Just imagine it. Don't question. An exact duplicate down to and including the cellular message units. This flesh would be imbued with all my memories and responses. Ask it a question you might ask me, and it would answer as I might answer. Even my mates wouldn't be able to distinguish between us.''

"So?" McKie said.

"Would there be any difference between us?" Tuluk asked.

"But you said . . .''

"There'd be one difference, wouldn't there?''

95

"The time element, the . . ."

"More than that," Tuluk said. "One would know it was a copy. Now, that chairdog in which Ser Bildoon sits is a different matter, not so?"

"Huh?"

"It's an unthinking animal," Tuluk said.

McKie stared at the chairdog Tuluk had indicated. It was a product of genetic shaping, gene surgery and selection. What possible difference could it make that a chairdog was an animal—however remotely descended?

"What does the chairdog eat?" Tuluk asked.

"The food tailored for it, what else?" McKie turned back to the Wreave, studied him.

"But neither the chairdog nor its food is the same as their ancestral flesh," Tuluk said. "The vat food is an endless, serial chain of protein. The chairdog is flesh which is ecstatic in its work."

"Of course! That's the way it was . . . made." McKie's eyes went wide. He began to see what Tuluk was explaining.

"The differences, these are the connectives," Tuluk said.

"McKie, do you understand this gibberish?" Bildoon demanded.

McKie tried to swallow in a dry throat. "The Caleban sees only these . . . *refined* differences?" he asked.

"And nothing else," Tuluk said.

"Then it doesn't see us as . . . shapes or dimensions or . . ."

"Or even as extensions in time the way we understand time," Tuluk said. "We are, perhaps, nodes on a standing wave. Time, for the Caleban, isn't something squeezed out of a tube. It's more like a line which your senses intersect."

"Hahhhhh," McKie breathed.

"I don't see where this helps us one bit," Bildoon said. "Our major problem is to find Abnethe. Do you have any idea, McKie, where that Caleban sent you?"

"I saw the constellations overhead," McKie said. "Before I leave, we'll get a mindcord on what I saw and have a computer check on the star patterns."

"Provided the pattern's in the master registry," Bildoon said.

"What about that slave culture McKie stumbled on?" one of the legal staff asked. "We could ask for a . . ."

"Haven't any of you been listening?" McKie asked. "Our problem is to find Abnethe. I thought we had her, but I'm beginning to think this may not be that easy. Where is she? How can we go into a court and say, 'At some unknown place in an unknown galaxy, a female believed to be Mliss Abnethe, but whom I didn't really see, is alleged to be conducting . . .' "

"Then what do we do?" the legal staffer growled.

"With Furuneo dead, who's watching Fanny Mae?" McKie asked.

"We have four enforcers inside, watching . . . where she is, and four outside, watching them," Bildoon said. "Are you sure you've no other clue to where you were?"

"None."

"A complaint by McKie would fail now," Bildoon said. "No—a better move might be to charge her with harboring a"—he shuddered—"a Pan Spechi fugitive."

"Do we know who that fugitive is?" McKie asked.

"Not yet. We haven't decided the proper course yet." He glanced at a Legal Department representative, a human female seated near Tuluk. "Hanaman?"

Hanaman cleared her throat. She was a fragile-looking woman, thick head of brown hair in gentle waves, long oval face with soft blue eyes, delicate nose and chin, wide full mouth.

"You think it advisable to discuss this in council now?" she asked.

"I do, or I wouldn't have called on you," Bildoon said.

For an instant McKie thought the reproof might bring real tears to Hanaman's eyes, then he saw the controlled downtwist at the corners of her mouth, the measuring stare she swept around the conference room. She had brains, he saw, and knew there were those here susceptible to her sex.

"McKie," she said, "is it necessary for you to stand on the table? You're not a Taprisiot."

"Thanks for reminding me," he said. He jumped down, found a chairdog opposite her, stared back at her with a bland intensity.

Presently she focused on Bildoon, said, "To bring everyone up to date, Abnethe with one Palenki tried to flog the Caleban about two hours ago. Acting on our orders, an enforcer prevented the flogging. He cut off the Palenki's arm with a raygen. As a result, Abnethe's legal staff is already seeking an injunction."

"Then they were prepared ahead of time," McKie said.

"Obviously," she agreed. "They're alleging outlaw sabotage, misfeasance by a bureau, mayhem, misconduct, malicious mischief, felonious misprision . . ."

"Misfeasance?" McKie demanded.

"This is a robo-legum case, not a Gowachin jurisdiction," Hanaman said. "We don't have to exonerate the prosecutor before entering the . . ." She broke off, shrugged. "Well, you know all that. BuSab is being held to answer for collective responsibility in the consequences of unlawful and wrongful acts committed by its agents in pursuance of the authority permitted them . . ."

"Wait a minute!" McKie interrupted. "This is bolder than I expected from that crowd."

"And they charge," Hanaman went on, "that the Bureau is guilty of a felony by criminal neglect in its failure to prevent a felony from being committed and in not bringing to justice the offender after such commission."

"Have they named names, or is it all John Does?" McKie asked.

"No names."

"If they're this bold, they're desperate," McKie said. "Why?"

"They know we aren't going to sit idly by and allow our people to be killed," Bildoon said. "They know we have copies of the contract with the Caleban, and it gives Abnethe sole control of the Caleban's jumpdoor. No one else could've been responsible for Furuneo's death, and the perpetrator . . ."

"No one except the Caleban," McKie said.

A profound silence settled over the room.

Presently Tuluk said, "You don't seriously believe . . ."

"No, I don't," McKie said. "But I couldn't prove my belief to a robo-legum court. This does present an interesting possibility, though." 98

"Furuneo's head," Bildoon said.

"Correct," McKie said. "We demand Furuneo's head."

"What if they contend the Caleban sequestered the head?" Hanaman asked.

"I don't intend asking them for it," McKie said. "I'm going to ask the Caleban."

Hanaman nodded, her gaze intent on McKie and with a light of admiration in her eyes. "Clever," she breathed. "If they attempt to interfere, they're guilty. But if we get the head . . ." She looked at Tuluk.

"What about it, Tuluk?" Bildoon asked. "Think you could get anything from Furuneo's brain?"

"That depends on how much time has passed between the death and our key-in, Tuluk said. "Nerve replay has limits, you know."

"We know," Bildoon said.

"Yeah," McKie said. "Only one thing for me to do now, isn't there?"

"Looks that way," Bildoon said.

"Will you call off the enforcers, or shall I?" McKie asked.

"Now, wait a minute!" Bildoon said. "I know you have to go back to that Beachball, but . . ."

"Alone," McKie said.

"Why?"

"I can give the demand for Furuneo's head in front of witnesses," McKie said, "but that's not enough. They *want* me. I got away from them, and they've no idea how much I know about their hidey hole."

"Exactly what do you know?" Bildoon asked.

"We've already been through that," McKie said.

"So you now see yourself as bait?"

"I wouldn't put it exactly that way," McKie said, "but if I'm alone, they might try bargaining with me. They might even . . ."

"They might even shorten you!" Bildoon snarled.

"You don't think it's worth the try?" McKie asked. He stared around the room at the attentive faces.

Hanaman cleared her throat. "I see a way out of this," she said.

Everyone looked at her.

"We could put McKie under Taprisiot surveillance," she said.

"He's a ready-made victim, if he's sitting there in a sniggertrance," Tuluk said.

"Not if the Taprisiot contacts are minimal every few seconds," she said.

"And as long as I'm not yelling for help, the Tappy breaks off," McKie said. "Good."

"I don't like it," Bildoon said. "What if . . ."

"You think they'll talk openly to me if they see the place full of enforcers?" McKie asked.

"No, but if we can prevent . . ."

"We can't, and you know it."

Bildoon glared at him.

"We must have those contacts between McKie and Abnethe, if we're going to try cross-charting to locate her position," Tuluk said.

Bildoon stared at the table in front of him.

"That Beachball has a fixed position on Cordiality," McKie argued. "Cordiality has a known planetary period. At the instant of each contact, the Ball will be pointing at a position in space—a line of least resistance for the contact. Enough contacts will describe a cone with . . ."

"With Abnethe somewhere in it," Bildoon supplied, looking up. "Provided you're right about this thing."

"The call connectives have to seek their conjunction through open space," Tuluk said. "There must be no large stellar masses between call points, no hydrogen clouds of any serious dimensions, no groups of large planetary . . ."

"I understand the theory," Bildoon said. "But there's no theory needed about what they can do to McKie. It'd take them less than two seconds to slip a jumpdoor over his neck and . . ." He drew a finger across his throat.

"So you have the Tappy contact me every two seconds," McKie said. "Work it in relays. Get a string of agents in. . . ."

"And what if they don't try to contact you?" Bildoon asked.

"Then we'll have to sabotage them," McKie said.

It is impossible to see any absolute through a screen of interpreters.

> **—Wreave Saying**

When you came right down to it, McKie decided, this Beachball wasn't as weird a home as some he'd seen. It was hot, yes, but that fitted a peculiar requirement of the occupant. Sentients existed in hotter climates. The giant spoon where the Caleban's *unpresence* could be detected—well, that could be equated with a divan. Wall handles, spools there, lights and whatnot—all those were almost conventional in appearance, although McKie seriously doubted he could understand their functions. The automated homes of Breedywie, though, displayed more outlandish control consoles.

The ceiling here was a bit low, but he could stand without stooping. The purple gloom was no stranger than the variglare of Gowachin, where most offworld sentients had to wear protective goggles while visiting friends. The Beachball's floor covering did not appear to be a conventional living organisim, but it *was* soft. Right now it smelled of a standard pyrocene cleaner-disinfectant, and the fumes were rather stifling in the heat.

McKie shook his head. The fly-buzz "zzzt" of Taprisiot contact every two seconds was annoying, but he found he could override the distraction.

"Your friend reached ultimate discontinuity," the Caleban had explained. "His substance has been removed."

For *substance* read blood-and-body, McKie translated. He hoped the translation achieved some degree of accuracy, but he cautioned himself not to be too sure of that.

If we could only have a little air current in here, McKie thought. *Just a small breeze.*

He mopped perspiration from his forehead, drank from

one of the water jugs he had provided for himself.

"You still there, Fanny Mae?" he asked.

"You observe my presence?"

"Almost."

"That *is* our mutual problem—seeing each other," the Caleban said.

"You're using time-ordinal verbs with more confidence, I note," McKie said.

"I get the hang of them, yes?"

"I hope so."

"I date the verb as a nodal position," the Caleban said.

"I don't believe I want that explained," McKie said.

"Very well; I comply."

"I'd like to try again to understand how the floggings are timed," McKie said.

"When shapes reach proper proportion," the Caleban said.

"You already said that. What shapes?"

"Already?" the Caleban asked. "That signifies earlier?"

"Earlier," McKie said. "That's right. You said that about shapes before."

"Earlier and before and already," the Caleban said. "Yes; times of different conjunction, by linear alteration of intersecting connectives."

Time, for the Caleban, is a position on a line, McKie reminded himself, recalling Tuluk's attempt at explanation. *I must look for the subtly refined differences; they're all this creature sees.*

"What shapes?" McKie repeated.

"Shapes defined by duration lines," the Caleban said. "I see many duration lines. You, oddly, carry visual sensation of one line only. Very strange. Other teachers explain this to self, but understanding fails . . . extreme constriction. Self admires molecular acceleration, but . . . maintenance exchange confuses."

Confuses! McKie thought.

"What molecular acceleration?" he asked.

"Teachers define molecule as smallest physical unit of element or compound. True?"

"That's right."

102

"This carries difficulty in understanding unless ascribed by self to perceptive difference between our species. Say, instead, molecule perhaps equals smallest physical unit visible to species. True?"

What's the difference? McKie thought. *It's all gibberish.* How had they gotten off onto molecules and acceleration from the proper proportion of undefined shapes?

"Why acceleration?" he insisted.

"Acceleration always occurs along convergence lines we use while speaking one to another."

Oh, damn! McKie thought. He lifted a water jug, drank, choked on a swallow. He bent forward, gasping. When he could manage it, he said, "The heat in here! Molecular speedup!"

"Do these concepts not interchange?" the Caleban asked.

"Never mind that!" McKie blurted, still spitting water. "When you speak to me . . . is *that* what accelerates the molecules?"

"Self assumes this true condition."

Carefully McKie put down the water jug, capped it. He began laughing.

"Not understand these terms," the Caleban objected.

McKie shook his head. The Caleban's words still came at him with that non-speech quality, but he detected definite querulous notes . . . overtones. Accents? He gave it up. There was *something,* though.

"Not understand!" the Caleban insisted.

This made McKie laugh all the harder. "Oh, my," he gasped, when he could catch his breath. "The ancient wheeze was right all along, and nobody knew it. Oh, my. Talk is just hot air!"

Again laughter convulsed him.

Presently he lay back, inhaled deeply. In a moment he sat up, took another swallow of water, capped the jug.

"Teach," the Caleban commanded. "Explain these unusual terms."

"Terms? Oh . . . certainly. Laughter. It's our common response to non-fatal surprise. No other significant communicative content."

"Laughter," the Caleban said. "Other nodal encounters with term noted."

"Other nodal . . ." McKie broke off. "You've heard the word before, you mean?"

"Before. Yes. I . . . self . . . I attempt understanding of term, laughter. We explore meaning now?"

"Let's not," McKie objected.

"Negative reply?" the Caleban asked.

"That's correct—negative. I'm much more curious about what you said about . . . maintenance exchange. That was what you said, wasn't it? Maintenance exchange confuses?"

"I attempt define position for you odd one-tracks," the Caleban said.

"One-tracks, that's how you think of us, eh?" McKie asked. He felt suddenly small and inadequate.

"Relationship of connectives one to many, many to one," the Caleban said. "Maintenance exchange."

"How in the hell did we get into this dead-end conversation?" McKie asked.

"You seek positional referents for placement of floggings, that begins conversation," the Caleban said.

"Placement . . . yeah."

"You understand S'eye effect?" the Caleban asked.

McKie exhaled slowly. To the best of his knowledge, no Caleban had ever before volunteered a discussion of the S'eye effect. The one-two-three of how to use the mechanism of the jumpdoors—yes, this was something they could (and did) explain. But the effect, the theory. . . .

"I . . . uh, use the jumpdoors," McKie said. "I know something of how the control mechanism is assembled and tuned to . . ."

"Mechanism not coincide with effect!"

"Uhhh, certainly," McKie agreed. "The word's not the thing."

"Precisement! We say—I translate, you understand?—we say, 'Term evades node.' You catch the hanging of this term, self thinks."

"I . . . uh, get the hang of it," McKie agreed.

"Recommend hang-line as good thought," the Caleban said. "Self, I believe we approach true communication. It wonders me."

"You wonder about it."

"Negative. It wonders about me."

104

"That's great," McKie said in a flat voice. "That's communication?"

"Understanding diffuses . . . . scatters? Yes—understanding scatters when we discuss connectives. I observe connectives of your . . . psyche. For psyche, I understand 'other self.' True?"

"Why not?" McKie asked.

"I see," the Caleban said, ignoring McKie's defeated tone, "psyche patterns, perhaps their colors. Approachments and outreaching touch by awareness. I come, through this, to unwinding of intelligence and perhaps understand what you mean by term, stellar mass. Self understands by being stellar mass, you hang this, McKie?"

"Hang this? Oh, sure . . . sure."

"Good! Comes now an understanding of your . . . wandering? Difficult word, McKie. Very likely this an uncertain exchange. Wandering equals movement along one line for you. This cannot exist for us. One moves, all move for Caleban on own plane. S'eye effect combines all movements and vision. I *see* you to other place of your desired wandering."

McKie, his interest renewed by this odd rambling, said, "You *see* us . . . that's what moves us from one place to another?"

"I hear sentient of your plane say sameness, McKie. Sentient say, 'I will see you to the door.' So? Seeing moves."

Seeing moves? McKie wondered. He mopped his forehead, his lips. It was so damned hot! What did all this have to do with "maintenance exchange"? Whatever that was!

"Stellar mass maintains and exchanges," the Caleban said. "Not see through *the* self. S'eye connective discontinues. You call this . . . privacy? Cannot say. This Caleban exists alone or self on your plane. Lonely."

We're all lonely, McKie thought.

And this universe would be lonely soon, if he couldn't find a way to escape their common grave. Why did the problem have to hang on such fumbling communication?

It was a peculiar kind of torment trying to talk to the Caleban under these pressures. He wanted to speed the processes of understanding, but speed sent all sentiency hurtling toward the brink. He could feel time flying past him. Urgency churned his stomach. He marched with time, retreated with it—and he'd started somehow on the wrong foot.

He thought about the fate of just one baby who'd never passed through a jumpdoor. The baby would cry . . . and there'd be no one to answer.

The awesome totality of the threat daunted him.

Everyone gone!

He put down a surge of irritation at the zzzt-beat of the Taprisiot intrusions. *That,* at least, was companionship.

"Do Taprisiots send our messages across space the same way?" he asked. "Do they *see* the calls?"

"Taprisiot very weak," the Caleban said. "Taprisiot not possess Caleban energy. Self energy, you understand?"

"I dunno. Maybe."

"Taprisiot see very thin, very short," the Caleban said. "Taprisiot not see through stellar mass of self. Sometimes Taprisiot ask for . . . boost? Amplification! Caleban provide service. Maintenance exchange, you hang? Taprisiot pay, we pay, you pay. All pay energy. You call energy demand . . . *hunger,* not so?"

"Oh, hell!" McKie said. "I'm not getting the half of . . ."

A brawny Palenki arm carrying a whip inserted itself into the space above the giant spoon. The whip cracked, sent a geyser of green sparks into the purple gloom. Arm and whip were gone before McKie could move.

"Fanny Mae," McKie whispered, "you still there?"

Silence . . . then, "No laughter, McKie. Thing you call surprise, but no laughter. I break line there. An abruptness, that flogging."

McKie exhaled, noted the mindclock timing of the incident, relayed the coordinates at the next Taprisiot contact.

There was no sense talking about pain, he thought. It was equally fruitless to explore inhaling whips or exhaling substance . . . or maintenance exchanges or hunger or stellar masses or Calebans moving other sentients by the energy of *seeing.* Communication was bogged down.

They'd achieved something, though Tuluk had been right. The S'eye contacts for the floggings required some timing or periodicity which could be identified. Perhaps there *was* a line of sight involved. One thing sure: Abnethe had her feet planted on a real planet somewhere. She and her mob of psycho friends—her *psycho-phants!*—all of them had a position in space which could be located. She had Palenkis, renegade Wreaves, an outlaw Pan Spechi—gods knew what all. She had Beautybarbers, too, and Taprisiots, probably. And somehow the Beautybarbers, the Taprisiots, and this Caleban all used the same sort of energy to do their work.

"Could we try again," McKie asked, "to locate Abnethe's planet?"

"Contract forbids."

"You have to honor it, eh? Even to the death?"

"Honor to ultimate discontinuity, yes."

"And that's pretty near, is it?"

"Position of ultimate discontinuity becomes visible to self," the Caleban said. "Perhaps this equates with near."

Again arm and whip flicked into being, showered the air with a cascade of green sparks, and withdrew.

McKie darted forward, stopped beside the spoon bowl. He had never before ventured quite this close to the Caleban. There was more heat near the bowl, and he felt a tingling sensation along his arms. The shower of green sparks had left no mark on the carpeting, no residual substance, nothing. McKie felt the insistent attraction of the Caleban's *unpresence,* a disturbing intensity this near. He forced himself to turn away. His palms were wet with fear.

What else am I afraid of here? he asked himself.

"Those two attacks came pretty close together," McKie said.

"Positional adjacency noted," the Caleban said. "Next coherence more distant. You say 'farther away'? True?"

"Yeah. Will the next flogging be your last?"

"Self not know," the Caleban said. "Your presence lessens flogging intensity. You . . . reject? Ahhh, repel!"

"No doubt," McKie said. "I wish I knew why the end of you means the end of everyone else."

"You transfer self of you with S'eye," the Caleban said. "So?"

"Everyone does!"

107

"Why? You teach explanation of this?"

"It's centralizing the whole damn universe. It's . . . it's created the specialized planets—honeymoon planets, gynecology planets, pediatrics planets, snow sport planets, geriatrics planets, swim sport planets, library planets—even BuSab has almost a whole planet to itself. Nobody gets by without it, anymore. Last figures I saw, fewer than a fraction of one percent of the sentient population had never used a S'eye jumpdoor."

"Truth. Such use creates connectives, McKie. You must hang this. Connectives must shatter with my discontinuity. Shatter conveys ultimate discontinuity for all who use jumpdoor S'eye."

"If you say so. I still don't understand."

"It occurs, McKie, because my fellows choose me for . . . coordinator? Inadequate term. Funnel? Handler, perhaps. No still inadequate. Ahhh! I, self of I, *am* S'eye!"

McKie backed away, retreating from such a wave of sadness that he felt he could not contain it. He wanted to scream in protest. Tears flowed down his cheeks unbidden. A sob choked him. Sadness! His body was reacting to it, but the emotion came from outside of himself.

Slowly it faded.

McKie blew air soundlessly through his lips. He still trembled from the passage of that emotion. It had been the Caleban's emotion, he realized. But it came out like the waves of heat in this room, swept over and immersed every nerve receptor in its path.

Sadness.

Responsibility for all those impending deaths, no doubt.

I am S'eye!

What in the name of all devils in the universe could the Caleban mean by such a strange claim? He thought of each jumpdoor passage. Connectives? Threads, perhaps. Each being caught by the S'eye effect trailed threads of itself through the jumpdoors. Was that it? Fanny Mae *had* used the word "funnel." Every traveler went through her . . . hands? Whatever. And when she ceased to exist, the threads broke. All died.

"Why weren't we warned about this when you offered us the S'eye effect?" McKie asked.

"Warned?"

"Yes! You offered . . ."

"Not offer. Fellows explain effect. Sentients of your wave expose great joy. They offer exchange of maintenance. You call this pay, not so?"

"We should've been warned."

"Why?"

"Well, you don't live forever, do you?"

"Explain this term, forever."

"Forever . . . always. Infinity?"

"Sentients of your wave seek infinity?"

"Not for individual members, but for . . ."

"Sentient species, they seek infinity?"

"Of course they do!"

"Why?"

"Doesn't everyone?"

"But what about other species for which yours must make way? You not believe in evolution?"

"Evo—" McKie shook his head sharply. "What's that have to do with it?"

"All beings have own day and depart," the Caleban said. "Day correct term? Day, unit of time, allotted linearity, normal extent of existence—you hang this?"

McKie's mouth moved, but no words came out.

"Length of line, time of existence," the Caleban said. "Approximately translated, correct?"

"But what gives you the right to . . . *terminate* us?" McKie demanded, finding his voice.

"Right not assumed, McKie," the Caleban said. "Given condition of proper connectives, another of my fellows takes up S'eye . . . control before self reaches ultimate discontinuity. Unusual . . . circumstance rejects such solution here. Mliss Abnethe and . . . associates shorten your one-track. My fellows leave."

"They ran for it while they had time; I understand," McKie said.

"Time . . . yes, your single-track line. This comparison provides suitable concept. Inadequate but sufficient."

"And you are definitely the last Caleban in our . . . wave?"

"Self alone," the Caleban said. "Terminal end-point

109

Caleban—yes. Self confirms description."

"Wasn't there any way to save yourself?" McKie asked.

"Save? Ahhh . . . avoid? Evade! Yes, evade ultimate discontinuity. This you suggest?"

"I'm asking if there wasn't some way for you to escape the way your . . . fellows did."

"Way exists, but result same for your wave."

"You could save yourself, but it would end us, that it?"

"You not possess honor concept?" the Caleban asked. "Save self, lose honor."

"Touché," McKie said.

"Explain touché," the Caleban said. "New term."

"Eh? Oh, that's a very old, ancient term."

"Linear beginning term, you say? Yes, those best with nodal frequency."

"Nodal frequency?"

"You say—often. Nodal frequency contains often."

"They mean the same thing; I see."

"Not same; similar."

"I stand corrected."

"Explain touché. What meaning conveys this term?"

"Meaning conveys . . . yeah. It's a fencing germ."

"Fencing? You signify containment?"

McKie explained fencing as best he could with a side journey into swordsmanship, the concept of single combat, competition.

"Effective touch!" the Caleban interrupted, her words conveying definite wonder. "Nodal intersection! Touché! Ahhh-ahhh! This contains why we find your species to fascinate us! This concept! Cutting line: touché! Pierced by meaning: touché!"

"Ultimate discontinuity," McKie snarled. "Touché! How far away is your next *touché* with the whip?"

"Intersection of whip touché!" the Caleban said. "You seek position of linear displacement, yes. It moves me. We perhaps occupy our linearities yet; but self suggests another species may need these dimensions. We leave, outgo from existence then. No so?"

When McKie didn't answer, the Caleban said, "McKie, you hang my meaning?"

"I think I'm going to sabotage you,'" McKie muttered.

Learning a language represents training in the delusions of that language.

—**Gowachin Aphorism**

Cheo, the ego-frozen Pan Spechi, stared out across the forest toward sunset over the sea. It was good, he thought, that the Ideal World contained such a sea. This tower Mliss had ordered built in a city of lesser buildings and spires commanded a view which included also the distant plain and far away mountains of the interior.

A steady wind blew against his left cheek, stirred his yellow hair. He wore green trousers and an open-mesh shirt of dull gold and gray. The clothing gave a subtle accent to his humanoid appearance, revealing the odd ripples of alien muscles here and there about his body.

An amused smile occupied his mouth, but not his eyes. He had Pan Spechi eyes, many-faceted, glistening—although the facets were edge-faded by his ego-surgery. The eyes watched the insect movements of various sentients on streets and bridgeways below him. At the same time, they reported on the sky overhead (a faraway flock of birds, streamers of sunset clouds) and told him of the view toward the sea and the nearby balustrade.

We're going to pull it off, he thought.

He glanced at the antique chronograph Mliss had given him. Crude thing, but it showed the sunset hour. They'd had to disengage from the Taprisiot mindclock system, though. This crude device showed two hours to go until the next contact. The S'eye controls would be more accurate, but he didn't want to move.

They can't stop us.

But maybe they can. . . .

He thought about McKie then. How had the BuSab agent found this place? And finding it, how had he come here?

McKie sat in the Beachball with the Caleban right now—bait, obviously. Bait!

For what?

Cheo did not enjoy the contradictory emotions surging back and forth through him. He had broken the most basic Pan Spechi law. He had captured his crèche's ego and abandoned his four mates to a mindless existence terminating in mindless death. A renegade surgeon's instruments had excised the organ which united the pentarchal Pan Spechi family across all space. The surgery had left a scar on Cheo's forehead and a scar on his soul, but he had never imagined he would find such delicate relish in the experience.

Nothing could take the ego from him!

But he was alone, too.

Death would end it, of course, but all creatures had that to face.

And thanks to Mliss, he had a retreat from which no other Pan Spechi could extricate him . . . unless . . . but there'd be no other Pan Spechi, very soon. There'd be no other organized sentients at all, except the handful Mliss had brought here to her Ark with its mad Boers and Blacks.

Abnethe came hurrying onto the observation deck behind him. His ears, as multiplanar in discrimination as his eyes, marked the emotions in her footsteps—boredom, worry, the constant fear which constricted her being.

Cheo turned.

She had been to a Beautybarber, he observed. Red hair now crowned her lovely face. McKie had red hair, too, Cheo reminded himself. She threw herself onto a reclining chairdog, stretched her legs.

"What's your hurry?" he asked.

"Those Beautybarbers!" she snapped. "They want to go *home!*"

"Send them."

"But where will I find others?"

"That *is* a proper problem, isn't it?"

"You're making fun of me, Cheo. Don't."

"Then tell them they can't go home."

"I did."

"Did you tell them why?"

112

"Of course not! What a thing to say!"

"You told Furuneo."

"I learned my lesson. Where are my legal people?"

"They've already gone."

"But I had other things to discuss with them!"

"Won't it wait?"

"You *knew* we had other business. Why'd you let them go?"

"Mliss, you don't really want to know the other matter on their minds."

"The Caleban's to blame," she said. "That's our story, and no one can disprove it. What was the other matter the legal numbheads wanted to discuss?"

"Mliss, drop it."

"Cheo!"

His Pan Spechi eyes glittered suddenly. "As you wish. They conveyed a demand from BuSab. They have asked the Caleban for Furuneo's head."

"His . . ." She paled. "But how did they know we . . ."

"It was an obvious move under the circumstances."

"What did you tell them?" she whispered. She stared at his face.

"I told them the Caleban closed the S'eye jumpdoor just as Furuneo was entering it of his own volition."

"But they know we have a monopoly on that S'eye," she said, her voice stronger. "Damn them!"

"Ahhh," Cheo said, "but Fanny Mae has been moving McKie and his friends around. *That* says we have no monopoly."

"That's exactly what I said before. Isn't it?"

"It gives us the perfect delaying tactic," he said. "Fanny Mae sent the head somewhere, and we don't know where. I've told her, of course, to deny this request."

She swallowed. "Is that . . . what you told them?"

"Of course."

"But if they question the Caleban . . ."

"They're just as likely to get a confusing answer as a usable one."

"That was very clever of you, Cheo."

"Isn't that why you keep me around?"

"I keep you around for mysterious reasons of my own," she said, smiling.

"I depend on that," he said.

"You know," she said, "I'll miss them."

"Miss who?"

"The ones who hunt us."

A basic requirement for BuSab agents is, perhaps, that we make the right mistakes.

—McKie's commentary on Furuneo, BuSab private files

Bildoon stood in the doorway to Tuluk's personal lab, his back to the long outer room where the Wreave's assistants did most of their work. The BuSab chief's deep-set eyes held a faceted glitter, a fire that failed to match the composure of his humanoid Pan Spechi face.

He felt weak and sad. He felt he existed in a contracting cave, a place without wind or stars. Time was closing in on everyone. Those he loved and those who loved him would die. All sentient love in the universe would die. The universe would become homeless, enclosed by melancholy.

Mourning filled his humanoid flesh: snows, leaves, suns—eternally alone.

He felt the demands of action, of decision, but feared the consequences of anything he might do. Whatever he touched might crumble, become so much dust falling through his fingers.

Tuluk, he saw, was working at a bench against the opposite wall. He had a length of the bullwhip's rawhide stretched between two clamps. Parallel with the rawhide and about a millimeter below it was a metal pole which lay balanced on air without visible support. Between rawhide and pole could be seen flickers of miniature lightning which danced along the entire length of the gap. Tuluk was bent over, reading meters set into the bench beneath the device.

"Am I interrupting anything?" Bildoon asked.

Tuluk turned a knob on the bench, waited, turned the knob once more. He caught the pole as the invisible supporting force released it. He racked the pole on supports against the back wall above the bench.

"That is a silly question," he said, turning.

"It is, at that," Bildoon said. "We have a problem."

"Without problems, we have no employment," Tuluk said.

"I don't think we're going to get Furuneo's head," Bildoon said.

"It's been so long now, we probably couldn't have gotten a reliable nerve replay, anyway," Tuluk said. He screwed his face slit into an S-curve, an expression he knew aroused amusement among other sentients but which represented intense thought for a Wreave. "What do the astronomers say about the star pattern McKie saw on that mysterious planet?"

"They think there may have been an error in the mindcord."

"Oh. Why?"

"For one thing, there isn't even a hint, not the slightest subjective indication of variation in stellar magnitudes."

"All the visible stars had the same light intensity?"

"Apparently."

"Odd."

"And the nearest pattern similarity," Bildoon said, "is one that doesn't exist anymore."

"What do you mean?"

"Well . . . there's a Big Dipper, a Little Dipper, various other constellations and zodiac similarities, but . . ." He shrugged.

Tuluk stared at him blankly. "I don't recognize the references," he said presently.

"Oh, yes—I forgot," Bildoon said. "We Pan Spechi, when we decided to copy human form, explored their history with some care. These patterns of stars are ones which were visible from their ancient homeworld."

"I see. Another oddity to go with what I've discovered about the material of this whip."

"What's that?"

"It's very strange. Parts of this leather betray a subatomic structure of peculiar alignment."

"Peculiar? How?"

"Aligned. Perfectly aligned. I've never seen anything like it outside certain rather fluid energy phenomena. It's as

116

though the material had been subjected to some peculiar force or stress. The result is, in some ways, similar to neomaser alignment of light quanta."

"Wouldn't that require enormous energy?"

"Presumably."

"But what could cause it?"

"I don't know. The interesting thing is that it doesn't appear to be a permanent change. The structure shows characteristics like plastic memory. It's slowly snapping back into reasonably familiar forms."

Bildoon heard the emphasis which betrayed Tuluk's disturbance. "Reasonably familiar?" he asked.

"That's another thing," Tuluk said. "Let me explain. These subatomic structures and their resultant overstructures of genetic message units undergo slow evolution. We can, by comparing structures, date some samples to within two or three thousand standard years. Since cattle cells form the basic protein for vat culture food, we have fairly complete records on them over a very long time indeed. The strange thing about the samples in this piece of rawhide"—he gestured with a mandibular extensor—"is that its pattern is very ancient."

"How ancient?"

"Perhaps several hundred thousand years."

Bildoon absorbed this for a moment, then, "But you told us earlier that this rawhide was only a couple of years old."

"According to our catalyzing tests, it is."

"Could this alignment stress have mixed up the pattern?"

"Conceivably."

"You doubt it, then?"

"I do."

"You're not trying to tell me that whip was brought forward through time?"

"I'm not trying to tell you anything outside the facts which I've reported. Two tests, previously considered reliable, do not agree as to the dating of this material."

"Time travel's an impossibility," Bildoon said.

"So we've always assumed."

"We *know* it. We know it mathematically and pragmatically. It's a fiction device, a myth, an amusing concept

117

employed by entertainers. We reject it, and we are left without paradox. Only one conclusion remains: The alignment stress, whatever that was, changed the pattern."

"If the rawhide were . . . squeezed through a subatomic filter of some sort, that might account for it," Tuluk said. "But since I have no such filter, nor the power to do this theoretical squeezing, I cannot test it."

"You must have some thoughts about it, though."

"I do. I cannot conceive of a filter which would do this thing without destroying the materials subjected to such forces."

"Then what you're saying," Bildoon said, voice rising in angry frustration, "is that an impossible device did an impossible thing to that impossible piece of . . . of . . .''

"Yes, sir," Tuluk said.

Bildoon noticed that Tuluk's aides in the outer room were turning their faces toward him, showing signs of amusement. He stepped fully into Tuluk's lab, closed the door.

"I came down here hoping you'd found something which might force their hand," Bildoon said, "and you give me conundrums."

"Your displeasure doesn't change the facts," Tuluk said.

"No, I guess it doesn't."

"The structure of the Palenki arm cells was aligned in a similar fashion," Tuluk said. "But only around the cut."

"You anticipated my next question."

"It was obvious. Passage through a jumpdoor doesn't account for it. We sent several of our people through jumpdoors with various materials and tested random cells—living and dead—for a check."

"Two conundrums in an hour is more than I like," Bildoon said.

"Two?"

"We now have twenty-eight positional incidents of Abnethe flogging that Caleban or attempting to flog it. That's enough to show us they do *not* define a cone in space. Unless she's jumping around from planet to planet, that theory's wrong."

"Given the powers of that S'eye, she *could* be jumping around."

"We don't think so. That isn't her way. She's a nesting bird. She likes a citadel. She's the kind who castles in chess when she doesn't have to."

"She could be sending her Palenkis."

"She's there with 'em every time."

"We've collected six whips and arms, in all," Tuluk said. "Do you want me to repeat these tests on all of them?"

Bildoon stared at the Wreave. The question wasn't like him. Tuluk was plodding, thorough.

"What would you rather be doing?" Bildoon asked.

"We have twenty-eight examples, you say. Twenty-eight is one of the euclidean perfects. It's four times the prime seven. The number strongly indicates randomness. But we're faced with a situation apparently excluding randomness. Ergo, an organizing pattern is at work which is not revealed by analytic numbering as far as we've taken it. I would like to subject the spacing—both in time and physical dimension— to a complete analysis, compare for any similarities we . . . ."

"You'd put an assistant on the other whips and arms to check them out?"

"That goes without saying."

Bildoon shook his head. "What Abnethe's doing—it's impossible!"

"If she does a thing, how can it be impossible?"

"They have to be somewhere!" Bildoon snapped.

"I find it very strange," Tuluk said, "this trait you share with humans of stating the obvious in such emphatic fashion."

"Oh, go to hell!" Bildoon said. He turned, slammed out of the lab.

Tuluk, racing to the door after him, opened it and called at the retreating back, "It is a Wreave belief that we already *are* in hell!"

He returned to his bench, muttering. Humans and Pan Spechi—impossible creatures. Except for McKie. Now, there was a human who occasionally achieved analytic rapport with sentients capable of higher logic. Well . . . every species had its exceptions to the norm.

119

If you say, "I understand." what have you done? You have made a value judgment.

—Laclac Riddle

By an effort of communication which he still did not completely understand, McKie had talked the Caleban into opening the Beachball's external port. This permitted a bath of spray-washed air to flow into the place where McKie sat. It also did one other thing: It allowed a crew of watchers outside to hold eye contact with him. He had just about given up hoping Abnethe would rise to the bait. There would have to be another solution. Visual contact with watchers also permitted a longer spacing between Taprisiot guard contacts. He found the new spacing less tiresome.

Morning sunshine splashed across the lip of the opening into the Beachball. McKie put a hand into the light, felt the warmth. He knew he should be moving around, making a poor target of himself, but the presence of the watchers made attack unlikely. Besides, he was tired, drugged to alertness and full of the odd emotions induced by *angeret.* Movement seemed an empty effort. If they wanted to kill him, they were going to do it. Furuneo's death proved that.

McKie felt a special pang at the thought of Furuneo's death. There had been something admirable and likable about the planetary agent. It had been a fumbling, pointless death—alone here, trapped. It had not advanced their search for Abnethe, only placed the whole conflict on a new footing of violence. It had shown the uncertainty of a single life—and through that life, the vulnerability of all life.

He felt a self-draining hate for Abnethe then. That madwoman!

He fought down a fit of trembling.

From where he sat McKie could see out across the lava shelf to the rocky palisades and a mossy carpeting of sea

120

growth exposed at the cliff base by the retreating tide.

"Suppose we have it all wrong," he said, speaking over his shoulder toward the Caleban. "Suppose we really aren't communicating with each other at all. What if we've just been making noises, assuming a communication content which doesn't exist?"

"I fail of understanding, McKie. The hang doesn't get me."

McKie turned slightly. The Caleban was doing something strange with the air around its position. The oval *stage* he had seen earlier shimmered once more into view, disappeared. A golden halo appeared at one side of the giant spoon, rose up like a smoke ring, crackled electrically, and vanished.

"We're assuming," McKie said, "that when you say something to me, I respond with meaningful words directly related to your statement—and that you do the same. This may not be the case at all."

"Unlikely."

"So it's unlikely. What *are* you doing there?"

"Doing?"

"All that activity around you."

"Attempt making self visible on your wave."

"Can you do it?"

"Possible."

A bell-shaped red glow formed above the spoon, stretched into a straight line, resumed its bell curve, began whirling like a child's jump rope.

"What see you?" the Caleban asked.

McKie described the whirling red rope.

"Very odd," the Caleban said. "I flex creativity, and you report visible sensation. You need yet that opening to exterior conditions."

"The open port? It makes it one helluva lot more comfortable in here."

"Comfort—concept self fails to understand."

"Does the opening prevent you from becoming visible?"

"It performs magnetic distraction, no more."

McKie shrugged. "How much more flogging can you take?"

"Explain much."

121

"You've left the track again," McKie said.

"Correct! That forms achievement, McKie."

"How is it an achievement?"

"Self leaves communicative track, and you achieve awareness of same."

"All right, that's an achievement. Where's Abnethe?"

"Contract . . ."

". . . prohibits revealing her location," McKie completed. "Maybe you can tell me, then, is she jumping around or remaining on one planet?"

"That helps you locate her?"

"How in fifty-seven hells do I know?"

"Probability smaller than fifty-seven elements," the Caleban said. "Abnethe occupies relatively static position on specific planet."

"But we can't find any pattern to her attacks on you or where they originate," McKie said.

"You cannot see connectives," the Caleban said.

The whirling red rope flickered in and out of existence above the giant spoon. Abruptly, it shifted color to a glowing yellow, vanished.

"You just disappeared," McKie said.

"Not my person visible," the Caleban said.

"How's that?"

"You not seeing person-self."

"That's what I said."

"Not say. Visibility to you not represent sameness of my person. You visible-see effect."

"I wasn't seeing you, eh? That was just some effect you created?"

"Correct."

"I didn't think it was you. You're going to be something more shapely. I do notice something though: There are moments when you use our verb tenses better; I even spotted some fairly normal constructions."

"Self hangs this get me," the Caleban said.

"Yeh, well . . . maybe you're not getting the hang of our language, after all." McKie stood up, stretched, moved closer to the open port, intending to peer out. As he moved, a shimmering silver loop dropped out of the air where he had been. He whirled in time to see it snake back through the small vortal tube of a jumpdoor.

"Abnethe, is that you?" McKie demanded.

There was no answer, and the jumpdoor snapped out of existence.

The enforcers watching from outside rushed to the port. One called, "You all right, McKie?"

McKie waved him to silence, took a raygen from his pocket, held it loosely in his hand. "Fanny Mae," he said, "are they trying to capture or kill me the way they did with Furuneo?"

"Observe theyness," the Caleban said. "Furuneo not having existence, observable intentions unknown."

"Did you see what just happened here?" McKie asked.

"Self contains awareness of S'eye employment, certain activity of employer persons. Activity ceases."

McKie rubbed his left hand across his neck. He wondered if he could bring the raygen into play quickly enough to cut any snare they might drop over his head. That silver thing dropping into the room had looked suspiciously like a noose.

"Is that how they got Furuneo?" McKie asked. "Did they drop a noose over his neck and pull him into the jumpdoor?"

"Discontinuity removes person of sameness," the Caleban said.

McKie shrugged, gave it up. That was more or less the answer they got every time they tried to question the Caleban about Furuneo's death.

Oddly, McKie discovered he was hungry. He whiped perspiration from his jaw and chin, cursed under his breath. There was no real assurance that what he *heard* in the Caleban's words represented real communication. Even granting some communication, how could he depend on the Caleban's interpretations or the Caleban's honesty? When the damn thing *spoke,* though, it radiated such a sense of sincerity that disbelief became almost impossible. McKie rubbed his chin, trying to catch an elusive thought. Strange. Here he was, hungry, angry, and afraid. There was no place to run. They had to solve this problem. He *knew* this for an absolute fact. Imperfect as communication with the Caleban actually was, the warning from the creature could not be ignored. Too many sentients had already died or gone insane.

He shook his head at the fly-buzz of Taprisiot contact.

Damn surveillance! This contact, however, failed to break off. It was Siker, the Laclac Director of Discretion. Siker had detected McKie's disturbed emotions and, instead of breaking contact, had locked in.

"No!" McKie raged. He felt himself stiffen into the mumbling sniggertrance. "No, Siker! Break off!"

"But what's wrong, McKie?"

"Break off, you idiot, or I'm done for!"

"Well . . . all right, but you felt . . ."

"Break it!"

Siker broke the contact.

Once more aware of his body, McKie found himself dangling from a noose which had choked off his breath and was pulling him up into a small jumpdoor. He heard scrambling at the open port. There were shouts, but he couldn't respond. Fire encircled his neck. His chest burned. Panic filled his mind. He found he had dropped the raygen during the sniggertrance. He was helpless. His hands clawed futilely at the noose.

Something grabbed his feet. Added weight tightened the noose.

Abruptly, the lifting force gave way. McKie, fell, sprawling in a tangle with whoever had grabbed his feet.

Several things happened at once. Enforcers helped him to his feet. A holoscan held by a Wreave was shoved past his face toward the jumpdoor, which closed with an electric snap. Groping hands and extensors removed the noose from his neck.

McKie inhaled a choking breath, gasped. He would have collapsed without the support of those around him.

Gradually, he became aware that five other sentients had entered the Beachball—two Wreaves, Laclac, a Pan Spechi and a human. The human and one of the Wreaves worked over McKie, clearing away the noose and supporting him. The holoscan operator was a Wreave, who was busy examining his instrument. The others were watching the space all around them, raygens ready. At least three sentients were trying to talk at the same time.

"All right!" McKie husked, shutting off the babble. His throat hurt when he spoke. He grabbed the length of noose from the Wreave's extensors, examined it. The rope was a silvery material which McKie failed to recognize. It had been cut cleanly with a raygen.

McKie looked at the enforcer with the holoscan, said, "What did you get?"

"The attack was made by an ego-frozen Pan Spechi, ser," the Wreave enforcer said "I got a good record of his face. We'll try for ID."

McKie tossed him the severed length of noose. "Get this thing back to the lab, too. Tell Tuluk to break it down to its basic structure. It may even have some of . . . Furuneo's cells on it. The rest of you . . ."

"Ser?" It was the Pan Spechi among the enforcers. "Yes?"

"Ser, we have orders. If an attempt is made on your life, we are to stay with you in here." He passed a raygen to McKie. "You dropped this, I believe."

McKie pocketed it with an angry gesture."

Taprisiot contact filled McKie's mind. "Break it!" he snapped.

But the contact firmed. It was Bildoon in a no-nonsense mood. "What's going on there, McKie?"

McKie explained.

"There are enforcers around you right now?"

"Yes."

"Anyone see the attackers?"

"We got a holoscan. It was the ego-frozen Pan Spechi."

McKie felt the emotional shudder from his Bureau chief. The sensation of horror was followed by a sharp command: "I want you back here at Central immediately."

"Look," McKie reasoned. "I'm the best bait we have. They want me dead for some . . ."

"Back, and now!" Bildoon said. "I'll have you brought in forcibly, if you make that necessary."

McKie subsided. He'd never before experienced such a black mood from a caller. "What's wrong?" he asked.

"You're bait wherever you are, McKie—there or here. If they want you, they'll come for you. I want you here, where we can surround you with guards."

"Something's happened," McKie said.

"You're damn right something's happened! All those bullwhips we were examining have disappeared. The lab is a shambles, and one of the Tuluk's assistants dead— decapitated and . . . no head."

"Ahhhhh, damn," McKie said. Then, "I'm on my way."

All the wisdom of the universe cannot match the alert willingness to dodge a violent blow.

—Ancient folk saying

Cheo sat cross-legged on a bare stretch of floor in the anteroom of his quarters. A sharply defined orange crosslight from windows in the next room stretched his shadow beside him like something lifeless from the night. In his hands he held the length of noose which had remained after it had been cut in the closing of the jumpdoor.

Damnable interference! That big Laclac with the raygen had been fast! And the Wreave with the holoscan had made a record through the jumpdoor—no doubt of that. They'd start hunting back along his trail now, asking questions, showing the holoscan of his face.

Not that it would do them any good.

Cheo's jeweled eyes glittered with shards of light. He could almost hear the BuSab operatives: *"Do you recognize this Pan Spechi?"*

The Pan Spechi equivalent of a chuckle, a rumbling grunt, shook him. Fat lot of good that search would do them! No friend or acquaintance from the old days would be likely to recognize his face, now that the medics had changed it. Oh, the bridge of the nose and the set of the eyes were similar, but . . .

Cheo shook his head. Why was he worrying? No one—absolutely no one—was going to stop him from destroying the Caleban! And after that, all these conjectures would be academic.

He sighed heavily. His hands were gripping the length of rope so tightly that his muscles ached. It took him several heartbeats of effort to release them. He climbed to his feet, threw the severed rope at a wall. A flailing end of it lashed a chairdog, which whimpered sibilantly through its atrophied vocal structure.

Cheo nodded to himself. They had to get the guards away from the Caleban or the Caleban away from the guards. He rubbed the scars on his forehead, hesitated. Was that a sound behind him? Slowly he turned, lowered his hand.

Mliss Abnethe stood in the doorway to the outer hall. The orange light created embers in the pearl sheathing of her gown. Her face held back anger, fear, and the grievous murmurings of her psyche.

"How long have you been there?" he asked, trying to keep his voice steady.

"Why?" She stepped into the room, closed the door. "What've you been doing?"

"Fishing," he said.

She swept the room with her insolent gaze, saw the pile of whips in a corner. They were thrown over something vaguely round and hairy. A wet red stain crept onto the floor from beneath the pile. She paled, whispered, "What's that?"

"Get out of here, Mliss," he said.

"What've you been doing?" she shrieked, whirling on him.

I should tell her, he thought. I should really tell her.

"I've been working to save our lives," he said.

"You've killed someone, haven't you?" she rasped.

"He didn't suffer," Cheo said, his voice tired.

"But you . . ."

"What's one more death among the quadrillions we're planning?" he asked. By all the devils of Gowachin, she was a tiresome bitch!

"Cheo, I'm afraid."

Why did she have to whimper like that?

"Calm yourself," he said. "I've a plan to separate the Caleban from her guardians. When we achieve that, we can proceed with her destruction, and the thing's done."

She swallowed, said, "She suffers. I know she does."

"That's nonsense! You've heard her deny it. She doesn't even know what pain means. No referents!"

"But what if we're wrong? What if it's just a misunderstanding?"

He advanced on her, stood glaring over her. "Mliss, do you have any idea how much *we'll* suffer if we fail?"

She shuddered. Presently, her voice almost normal, she asked, "What's your plan?"

One species can, all by itself, produce infinite varieties of experiences. The interaction between many species creates the illusion that infinity has been enlarged by several orders of magnitude.

—The Caleban Question
by Dwel Hartavid

McKie felt danger signals from every nerve ending. He stood with Tuluk in the Wreave's lab. The place should have been comfortingly familiar, but McKie felt as though the walls had been removed, opening the lab onto boundless space from which attack could come. No matter which way he turned, his back was exposed to menace. Abnethe and her friends were getting desperate. The fact of desperation said she was vulnerable. If only he could understand her vulnerability. Where was she vulnerable? What was her weakness?

And where had she hidden herself?

"This is very strange material," Tuluk said, straightening from the bench where he had been examining the silvery rope. "Very strange."

"What's strange about it?"

"It cannot exist."

"But it's right there." McKie pointed.

"I can see that, my friend."

Tuluk extruded a single mandible, scratched thoughtfully at the right lip of his face slit. One orange eye became visible as he turned, glanced at McKie.

"Well?" McKie said.

"The only planet where this material could have been grown ceased to exist several millennia ago," Tuluk said. "There was only one place—a peculiar combination of chemistry and solar energy . . ."

"You've got to be mistaken! The stuff's right there."

"The Archer's Eye," Tuluk said. "You recall the story of the nova there?"

McKie cocked his head to one side, thought for a moment, then, "I've read about it, yes,"

"The planet was called Rap," Tuluk said. "This is a length of Rapvine."

"Rapvine."

"You've heard of it?"

"I don't believe so."

"Yes, well . . . it's strange stuff. Has a relatively short life span, among its other peculiar characteristics. Another thing: the ends don't fray, even when it's cut. See?" Tuluk plucked several strands from the cut end, released them. They slapped back into position. "It was called *intrinsic attraction*. There's been considerable speculation about it. I'm now in a position to . . ."

"Short life," McKie interrupted. "How short?"

"No more than fifteen or twenty standard years under the most ideal conditions."

"But the planet . . ."

"Milennia ago, yes."

McKie shook his head to clear it. His eyes scanned the length of silvery rope suspiciously. "Obviously, somebody found how to grow the stuff someplace other than Rap."

"Perhaps. But they've managed to keep it a secret all this time."

"I don't like what I think you're thinking," McKie said.

"That's the most convoluted statement I've ever heard you make," Tuluk said. "Its meaning is clear enough, however. You believe I'm considering the possibility of time travel or . . ."

"Impossible!" McKie snapped.

"I've been engaged in a most interesting mathematical analysis of this problem," Tuluk said.

"Number games aren't going to help us."

"Your behavior is most un-McKie," Tuluk said. "Irrational. Therefore, I'll try not to burden your mind with too much of my symbolic construction. It is, however, more than a game for . . ."

"Time travel," McKie said. "Nonsense!"

131

"Our habitual forms of perception tend to interfere with the thinking process required for analysis of this problem," Tuluk said. "Thus, I discard these modes of thought."

"Such as?"

"If we examine the series relationships, what do we have? We have a number of point-dimensions in space. Abnethe occupies a position on a specific planet, as does the Caleban. We are given the actuality of contact between the two points, a series of events."

"So?"

"We must assume a pattern to these point-contacts."

"Why? They could be random examp—"

"Two specific planets whose movements describe coherent patterns in space. A pattern, a rhythm. Otherwise, Abnethe and her crew would be attacking with more frequency. We are confronted by a system which defies conventional analysis. It had temporal rhythm translatable into point-series rhythm. It is spatial and temporal."

McKie felt the attraction of Tuluk's argument as a force lifting his mind out of a cloud. "Some form of reflection, maybe?" he asked. "It doesn't have to be time trav—"

"This is not a fugue!" Tuluk objected. "A simple quadratic equation achieves no elliptical functions here. Ergo we are dealing with linear relationships."

"Lines," McKie whispered. "Connectives."

"Eh? Oh, yes. Linear relationships which describe moving surfaces across some form or forms of dimension. We cannot be sure of the Caleban's dimensional outlook, but our own is another matter."

McKie pursed his lips. Tuluk had moved into an extremely thin air of abstractions, but there was an inescapable elegance to the Wreave's argument.

"We can treat all forms of space as quantities determined by other quantities," Tuluk said. "We have methods for dealing with such forms when we wish to solve for unknowns."

"Ahhh," McKie murmured. "N-dimension points."

"Precisely. We first consider our data as a series of measurements which define the space between such points."

132

McKie nodded. "A classic n-fold extended aggregate."

"Now you begin to sound like the McKie familiar to me. An aggregate of n dimensions, to be sure. And what is time in such a problem? Time we know to be an aggregate of one dimension. But we are given, you'll recall, a number of point-dimensions in space *and* time."

McKie whistled soundlessly, admiring the Wreave's logic, then, "We either have one continuous variable in the problem or n continuous variables. Beautiful!"

"Just so. And by reduction through the infinity calculus, we discover we are dealing with two systems containing n-body properties."

"That's what you found?"

"That's what I found. It can only follow that the point-contacts of our problem have their separate existence within different frameworks of time. Ergo, Abnethe occupies another dimension time from that of the Beachball. Inescapable conclusion."

"We may not be dealing with time travel phenomena in the classic fictional sense," McKie said.

"These subtle differences the Caleban sees," McKie said. "These *connectives,* these threads . . ."

"Spiderwebs embedded in many universes," Tuluk said. "Perhaps. Let's assume individual lives spin these web threads . . ."

"Movements of matter undoubtedly spin them, too."

"Agreed. And they cross. They unite. They intersect. They combine in mysterious ways. They become tangled. Some of the web threads are stronger than others. I have experienced this entanglement, you know, when I placed the call which saved your life. I can imagine some of these threads being rewoven, combined, aligned—what have you—to recreate conditions of long past times in our dimensions. Might be a relatively simple problem for a Caleban. The Caleban might not even understand the recreation the way we do."

"I'll buy that."

"What would it take?" Tuluk mused. "A certain poignancy of experience, perhaps; something which imparts sufficient strength to the lines, threads, webs of the past that they

133

can be picked up, manipulated to reproduce the original setting and its contents.''

"We're just tossing words back and forth," McKie objected. "How could you reweave an entire planet or the space around . . ."

"Why not? What do we know of the powers involved? To a crawling insect, three of your strides may be a day's journey.''

McKie felt himself being convinced in spite of native caution. "It is true," he agreed, "that the Caleban S'eye gives us the power to walk across light years."

"Such a common exploit that we no longer even wonder at the enormous energies this must require. Think what such a journey would mean to our hypothetical insect! And we may be getting the merest glimpse of Caleban powers.''

"We should never have accepted the S'eye," McKie said. "We had perfectly adequate FTL ships and metabolic suspension. We should've told the Calebans to go jump in their collective connectives!''

"And deny ourselves real-time control of our universe? Not on your life, McKie. What we should have done was test the gift first. We should have probed for dangers. We were too bedazzled by it, though.''

McKie lifted his left hand to scratch his eyebrow, felt a prickling of danger. It rushed up his spine, exploded in a blow against his arm. He felt pain there; something bit through to the bone. Despite the shock, he whirled, saw a Palenki arm upraised with a glittering blade. The arm came through a narrow vortal tube. Visible through the opening were a Palenki turtle head, beside it, the right side of a Pan Spechi face—purple scar on the forehead, one faceted emerald eye.

For a suspended moment McKie saw the blade begin its descent toward his face, knew it was going to strike before his shocked muscles could respond. He felt metal touch his forehead, saw the orange glow of a raygen beam stab past his face.

McKie stood frozen, locked in stillness. It was a tableau. He saw surprise on the Pan Spechi face, saw a severed Palenki arm begin its tumble to the floor still clutching a shattered metal remnant. McKie's heart was pounding as

134

though he had been running for an hour. He felt hot wetness spread across his left temple. It ran down his cheek, along his jaw, into his collar. His arm throbbed, and he saw blood dripping from his fingertips.

The S'eye jumpdoor had winked out of existence.

Someone was beside him then, pressing a compress against his head where the metal had touched . . .

Touched?

Once more he had prepared himself for sudden death at a Palenki's hand, a descending blade. . . .

Tuluk, he saw, was bending to retrieve the metal remnant.

"That's another nick of time I've escaped," McKie said.

Surprisingly, there was no tremor in his voice.

Providence and Manifest Destiny are synonyms often invoked to support arguments founded in wishful thinking.

—from The Wreave Commentary

It was midafternoon on Central before Tuluk sent for McKie to return to the lab. Two squads of enforcers accompanied McKie. There were enforcers all around in augmented force. They watched the air, the walls, the floors. They watched each other and the space around their alternate numbers. Every sentient carried a raygen at the ready.

McKie, having spent two hours with Hanaman and five of her aides in Legal, was ready for down-to-dirt facts. Legal was moving to search every Abnethe property, to seize every record they could find—but it was all off there somewhere in the rarefied atmosphere of symbols. Perhaps something would come of it, though. They had a telocourt order, reproduced thousands of times, giving the Bureau's enforcement arm sufficient authority for search on most worlds outside the Gowachin pale. Gowachin officials were moving in their own way to cooperate—exonerating sufficient enforcers, clearing the names of appropriate police agencies.

Crime-One police on Central and elsewhere were assisting. They had provided enforcers, opened files normally not privileged to BuSab, temporarily linked their identifcation and modus computers to BuSab's core.

It was action, of course, but it struck McKie as too circuitous, too abstract. They needed another kind of line to Abnethe, something connected to her which could be reeled in despite any of her attempts to escape.

He felt now that he lived in a flushed-out spirit.

Nooses, blades, gnashing jumpdoors—there was no mercy in the conflict which engaged them.

Nothing he did slowed the dark hurricane that hurtled

toward the sentient universe. His nerves punished him with sensations of rough, grasping inadequacy. The universe returned a glassy stare, full of his own fatigue. The Caleban's words haunted him—*self-energy . . . seeing moves . . . I am S'eye!*

Eight enforcers had crowded into the small lab with Tuluk. They were being very self effacing, apologetic—evidence that Tuluk had protested in that bitingly sarcastic way Wreaves had.

Tuluk glanced up at McKie's entrance, returned to examination of a metal sliver held in stasis by a subtron field beneath a bank of multicolored lights on his bench.

"Fascinating stuff, this steel," he said, lowering his head to permit one of his shorter and more delicate mandibular extensors to get a better grip on a probe with which he was tapping the metal.

"So it's steel," McKie said, watching the operation.

Each time Tuluk tapped the metal, it gave off a shimmering spray of purple sparks. They reminded McKie of something just at the edge of memory. He couldn't quite place the association. A shower of sparks. He shook his head.

"There's a chart down the bench," Tuluk said. "You might have a look at it while I finish here."

McKie glanced to his right, saw an oblong of chalf paper with writing on it. He moved the necessary two steps to reach the paper, picked it up, studied it. The writing was in Tuluk's neat script.

Substance: steel, an iron-base alloy. Sample contains small amts manganese, carbon, sulfur, phosphorus, and silicon, some nickel, zirconium, and tungsten with admixture chromium, molybdenum, and vanadium.

Source comparison: matches Second-Age steel used by human political subunit Japan in making of swords for Samurai Revival.

Tempering: sample hard-quenched on cutting edge only; back of sword remains soft.

Estimated length of original artifact: 1.01 meters.

Handle: linen cord wrapped over bone and lacquered. (See lacquer, bone, and cord analyses: attached.)

McKie glanced at the attached sheet: "Bone from a sea mammal's tooth, reworked after use on some other artifact, nature unknown but containing bronze."

The linen cord's analysis was interesting. It was of relatively recent manufacture, and it displayed the same submolecular characteristics as the earlier samples of rawhide.

The lacquer was even more interesting. It was based in an evaporative solvent which was identified as a coal-tar derivative, but the purified sap was from an ancient *Coccus lacca* insect extinct for millennia.

"You get to the part about the lacquer yet?" Tuluk asked, glancing up and twisting his face slit aside to look at McKie.

"Yes."

"What do you think of my theory now?"

"I'll believe anything that works," McKie growled.

"How are your wounds?" Tuluk asked, returning to his examination of the metal.

"I'll recover." McKie touched the omniflesh patch at his temple. "What's that you're doing now?"

"This material was fashioned by hammering," Tuluk said, not looking up. "I'm reconstructing the pattern of the blows which shaped it." He shut off the stasis field, caught the metal deftly in an extended mandible.

"Why?"

Tuluk tossed the metal onto the bench, racked the probe, faced McKie.

"Manufacture of swords such as this was a jealously guarded craft," he said. "It was handed down in families, father to son, for centuries. The irregularity of the hammer blows used by each artisan followed characteristic patterns to an extent that the maker can be identified without question by sampling that pattern. Collectors developed the method to verify authenticity. It's as definite as an eye print, more positive than any skin-print anomaly."

"So what did you find out?"

"I ran the test twice," Tuluk said, "to be certain. Despite the fact that cell revivification tests on lacquer and cord attachments show this sword to have been manufactured no more than eighty years ago, the steel was fashioned by an artisan dead more thousands of years than I care to contemplate. His name was Kanemura, and I can give you the index referents to verify this. There's no doubt who made that sword."

The interphone above Tuluk's bench chimed twice, and the face of Hanaman from Legal appeared on it. "Oh, there you are, McKie," she said, peering past Tuluk.

"What now?" McKie asked, his mind still dazed by Tuluk's statement.

"We've managed to get those injunctions," she said. "They lock up Abnethe's wealth and production on every sentient world except the Gowachin."

"But what about the warrants?" McKie demanded.

"Of course; those, too," Hanaman said. "That's why I'm calling. You asked to be notified immediately."

"Are the Gowachin cooperating?"

"They've agreed to declaration of a ConSent emergency in their jurisdiction. That allows all Federation police and BuSab agencies to act there for apprehension of suspects."

"Fine," McKie said. "Now, if you could only tell me when to find her, I think we can pick her up."

Hanaman looked from the screen with a puzzled frown. "When?"

"Yeah," McKie snarled. "When."

If you believe yourself sufficiently hungry, you will eat your own thoughts.

—A Palenki Saying

The report on the Palenki phylum pattern was waiting for McKie when he returned to Bildoon's office for their strategy conference. The conference had been scheduled earlier that day and postponed twice. It was almost midnight at Central, but most of the Bureau's people remained on duty, especially the enforcers. *Sta-lert* capsules had been issued along with the *angeret* by the medical staff. The enforcer squad accompanying McKie walked with that edgy abruptness this mixture of chemicals always exacted as payment.

Bildroon's chairdog had lifted a footrest and was ripple-massaging the Bureau Chief's back when McKie entered the office. Opening one jeweled eye, Bildoon said, "We got the report on the Palenki—the shell pattern you holoscanned." He closed his eye, sighed. "It's on my desk there."

McKie patted a chairdog into place, said, "I'm tired of reading. What's it say?"

"Shipsong Phylum," Bildoon said. "Positive identification. Ahhh, friend—I'm tired, too."

"So?" McKie said. He was tempted to signal for a masage from the chairdog. Watching Bildoon made it very attractive. But McKie knew this might put him to sleep. The enforcers moving restlessly around the room must be just as tired as he was. They'd be sure to resent it if he popped off for a nap.

"We got warrants and picked up the Shipsong Phylum's leader," Bildoon said. "It claims every phylum associate is accounted for."

"True?"

"We're trying to check it, but how can you be sure? They keep no written records. It's just a Palenki's word, whatever that's worth."

"Sworn by its arm, too, no doubt," McKie said.

"Of course." Bildoon stopped the chairdog massage, sat up. "It's true that phylum identification patterns can be used illegitimately."

"It takes a Palenki three or four weeks to regrow an arm," McKie said.

"What's that signify?"

"She must have several dozen Palenkis in reserve."

"She could have a million of 'em for all we know."

"Did this phylum leader resent its pattern being used by an unauthorized Palenki?"

"Not that we could see."

"It was lying," McKie said.

"How do you know?"

"According to the Gowachin juris-dictum, phylum forgery is one of the eight Palenki capital offenses. And the Gowachin should know, because they were assigned to educate the Palenkis in acceptable law when R&R brought those one-armed turtles into the ConSent fold."

"Huh!" Bildoon said. "How come Legal didn't know that? I've had them researching this from the beginning."

"Privileged legal datum," McKie said. "Interspecies courtesy and all that. You know how the Gowachin are about individual dignity, privacy, that sort of thing."

"You'll be read out of their court when they find out you spilled this," Bildoon said.

"No. They'll just appoint me prosecutor for the next ten or so capital cases in their jurisdiction. If the prosecutor accepts a case and fails to get a conviction, he's the one they execute, you know."

"And if you decline the cases?"

"Depends on the case. I could draw anything from a one-to-twenty sentence for some of them."

"One-to—you mean standard years?"

"I don't mean minutes," McKie growled.

"Then why'd you tell me?"

"I want you to let me break this phylum leader."

"Break him? How?"

"You any idea how important the mystique of the arm is to the Palenki?"

141

"Some idea. Why?"

"Some idea," McKie muttered. "Back in the primitive days, Palenkis made criminals eat their arms, then inhibited regrowth. Much loss of face, but even greater injury to something very deep and emotional for the Palenkis."

"You're not seriously suggesting . . ."

"Of course not!"

Bildoon shuddered. "You humans have a basically bloodthirsty nature. Sometimes I think we don't understand you."

"Where's this Palenki?" McKie asked.

"What're you going to do?"

"Question him! What'd you think?"

"After what you just said, I wasn't sure."

"Come off that, Bildoon. Hey, you!" McKie gestured to a Wreave enforcer lieutenant. "Bring the Palenki in here."

The enforcer glanced at Bildoon.

"Do as he says," Bildoon said.

The enforcer looped his mandibles uncertainly but turned and left the room, signaling half a squad to attend him.

Ten minutes later the Palenki phylum leader was herded into Bildoon's office. McKie recognized the snake-weaving pattern on the Palenki's carapace, nodded to himself: Shipsong Phylum, all right. Now that he saw it, he made the identification himself.

The Palenki's multiple legs winked to a stop in front of McKie. The turtle face turned toward him expectantly. "Will you truly make me eat my arm?" it asked.

McKie glanced accusingly at the Wreave lieutenant.

"It asked what kind of human you were," the Wreave explained.

"I'm glad you rendered such an accurate description," McKie said. He faced the Palenki. "What do *you* think?"

"I think not possible, Ser McKie. Sentients no longer permit such barbarities." The turtle mouth rendered the words without emotion, but the arm dangling to the right from its headtop juncture writhed with uncertainty.

"I may do something worse," McKie said.

"What is worse?" the Palenki asked.

"We'll see, won't we? Now! You can account for every member of your phylum, is that what you claim?"

"That is correct."

"You're lying," McKie said, voice flat.

"No!"

"What's your phylum name?" McKie asked.

"I give that only to phylum brothers!"

"Or to the Gowachin," McKie said.

"You are not Gowachin."

In a flat splatting of Gowachin grunts, McKie began describing the Palenki's probable unsavory ancestry, its evil habits, possible punishments for its behavior. He concluded with the Gowachin identification-burst, the unique emotion/word pattern by which he was required to identify himself before the Gowachin bar.

Presently the Palenki said, "You are the human they admitted to their legal concourse. I've heard about you."

"What's your phylum name?" McKie demanded.

"I am called Biredch of Ank," the Palenki said, and there was a resigned tone in its voice.

"Well, Biredch of Ank, you're a liar."

"No!" the arm writhed.

There was terror in the Palenki's manner now. It was a brand of fear McKie had been trained to recognize in his dealings through the Gowachin. He possessed the Palenki's privileged name; he could demand the arm.

"You have compounded a capital offense," McKie said.

"No! No! No!" the Palenki protested.

"What the other sentients in this room don't realize," McKie said, "is that phylum brothers accept gene surgery to affix the identity pattern on their carapaces. The index marks are grown into the shell. Isn't this true?"

The Palenki remained silent.

"It's true," McKie said. He noted that the enforcers had moved into a close ring around them, fascinated by this encounter. "You!" McKie said, snapping an arm toward the Wreave lieutenant. "Get your men on their toes!"

"Toes?"

"They should be watching every corner of this room," McKie said. "You want Abnethe to kill our witness?"

Abashed, the lieutenant turned, barked orders to his squad, but the enforcers were already at their shifty, turning, eye-

143

darting inspection of the room. The Wreave lieutenant shook a mandible angrily, fell silent.

McKie returned his attention to the Palenki. "Now, Biredch of Ank, I'm going to ask you some special questions. I already know the answers to some of them. If I catch you in one lie, I'll consider a reversion to barbarism. Too much is at stake here. Do you understand me?"

"Ser, you cannot believe that . . ."

"Which of your phylum mates did you sell into slave service with Mliss Abnethe?" McKie demanded.

"Slaving is a capital offense," the Palenki breathed.

"I've already said you were implicated in a capital offense," McKie said. "Answer the question."

"You ask me to condemn myself?"

"How much did she pay you?" McKie asked.

"Who pay me what?"

"How much did Abnethe pay you?"

"For what?"

"For your phylum mates?"

"What phylum mates?"

"That's the question," McKie said. "I want to know how many you sold, how much you were paid, and where Abnethe took them."

"You cannot be serious!"

"I'm recording this conversation," McKie said. "I'm going to call your United Phyla Council presently, play the recording for them, and suggest they deal with you."

"They will laugh at you! What evidence could you . . ."

"I've your own guilty voice," McKie said. "We'll get a voicecorder analysis of everything you've said and submit it with the recording to your council."

"Voicecorder? What is this?"

"It's a device which analyzes the subtle pitch and intonation of the voice to determine which statements are true and which are false."

"I've never heard of such a device!"

"Damn few sentients know all the devices BuSab agents use," McKie said. "Now, I'm giving you one more chance. How many of your mates did you sell?"

"Why are you doing this to me? What is so important

144

about Abnethe that you should ignore every interspecies courtesy, deny me the rights of . . ."

"I'm trying to save your life," McKie said.

"Now who's lying?"

"Unless we find and stop Abnethe," McKie said, "damn near every sentient in our universe excepting a few newly hatched chicks will die. And *they'll* stand almost no chance without adult protection. You've my oath on it."

"Is that a solemn oath?"

"By the *egg* of my arm," McKie said.

"Ooooooo," the Palenki moaned. "You know even this of the egg?"

"I'm going to invoke your name and force you to swear by your most solemn oath in just a moment," McKie said.

"I've sworn by my arm!"

"Not by the *egg* of your arm," McKie said.

The Palenki lowered its head. The single arm writhed.

"How many did you sell?" McKie asked.

"Only forty-five," the Palenki hissed.

"*Only* forty-five?"

"That's all! I swear it!" Glistening fear oils began oozing from the Palenki's eyes. "She offered so much, and the chosen ones accepted freely. She promised unlimited eggs!"

"No breeding limit?" McKie asked. "How could that be?"

The Palenki glanced fearfully at Bildoon, who sat hunched across the desk, face grim.

"She would not explain, other than to say she'd found new worlds beyond the ConSent jurisdiction."

"Where are those worlds?" McKie asked.

"I don't know! I swear it by the egg of my arm! I don't know!"

"How was the deal set up?" McKie asked.

"There was a Pan Spechi."

"What did he do?"

"He offered my phylum the profits from twenty worlds for one hundred standard years."

"Whoooeee!" someone behind McKie said.

"When and where did this transaction take place?" McKie asked.

"In the home of my eggs only a year ago."

"A hundred years' profits," McKie muttered. "A safe deal. You and your phylum won't be around even a fraction that long if she succeeds in what she's planning."

"I didn't know. I swear I didn't know. What is she doing?"

McKie ignored the question, asked, "Have you any clue at all as to where her worlds may be?"

"I swear not," the Palenki said. "Bring your voicecorder. It will prove I speak the truth."

"There's no such thing as a voicecorder for your species," McKie said.

The Palenki stared at him a moment, then, "May your eggs rot!"

"Describe the Pan Spechi for us," McKie said.

"I withdraw my cooperation!"

"You're in too far now," McKie said, "and my deal's the only one in town."

"Deal?"

"If you cooperate, everyone in this room will forget your admission of guilt."

"More trickery," the Palenki snarled.

McKie looked at Bildoon, said, "I think we'd better call in the Palenki council and give them the full report."

"I think so," Bildoon agreed.

"Wait!" the Palenki said. "How do I know I can trust you?"

"You don't," McKie said.

"But I have no choice, is that what you say?"

"That's what I say."

"May your eggs rot if you betray me."

"Every one of them," McKie agreed. "Describe your Pan Spechi."

"He was ego-frozen," the Palenki said. "I saw the scars, and he bragged of it to show that I could trust him."

"Describe him."

"One Pan Spechi looks much like another. I don't know—but the scars were purple. I remember that."

"Did he have a name?"

"He was called Cheo."

McKie glanced at Bildoon.

"The name signifies new meanings for old ideas," Bildoon said. "It's in one of our ancient dialects. Obviously an alias."

McKie returned his attention to the Palenki. "What kind of agreement did he give you?"

"Agreement?"

"Contract . . . surety! How did he insure the payoff?"

"Oh. He appointed phylum mates of my selection as managers on the chosen worlds."

"Neat," McKie said. "Simple hiring agreements. Who could fault a deal like that or prove anything by it?"

McKie brought out his toolkit, removed the holoscan, set it for projection, and dialed the record he wanted. Presently the scan which the Wreave enforcer had captured through the jumpdoor danced in the air near the Palenki. McKie slowly turned the projection full circle, giving the Palenki a chance to see the face from every angle.

"Is that Cheo?" he asked.

"The scars present the identical pattern. It is the same one."

"That's a valid ID," McKie said, glancing at Bildoon. "Palenkis can identify random line patterns better than any other species in the universe."

"Our phylum patterns are extremely complex," the Palenki boasted.

"We know," McKie said.

"What good does this do us?" Bildoon asked.

"I wish I knew," McKie said.

No language has ever really come to grips with temporal relationships.

—A Gowachin Opinion

McKie and Tuluk were arguing about the time-regeneration theory, ignoring the squad of enforcers guarding them, although it was obvious their companions found the argument interesting.

The theory was all over the Bureau by this time—about six hours after the session with the Palenki phylum leader, Biredch of Ank. It had about as many scoffers as it had supporters.

At McKie's insistence, they had taken over one of the interspecies training rooms, had set up a datascan console, and were trying to square Tuluk's theory with the subatomic alignment phenomenon discovered in the rawhide and other organic materials captured from Abnethe.

It was Tuluk's thought that the alignment might point toward some spatial vector, giving a clue to Abnethe's hideout.

"There must be some vector of focus in our dimension," Tuluk insisted.

"Even if that's true, what good would it do us?" McKie asked. "She's not in our dimension. I say we go back to the Caleban's . . ."

"You heard Bildoon. You don't go anywhere. We leave the Beachball to enforcers while we concentrate on . . ."

"But Fanny Mae's our only source of new data!"

"Fanny . . . oh, yes; the Caleban."

Tuluk was a pacer. He had staked out an oval route near the room's instruction focus, tucked his mandibles neatly into the lower fold of his facial slit, and left only his eyes and breathing/speech orifice exposed. The flexing bifurcation which served him as legs carried him around a chairdog occupied by McKie, thence to a point near a Laclac enforcer at one extreme of the instruction focus, thence back along a mixed line of enforcers who milled around across from a float-table on which McKie was doodling, thence around behind McKie and back over the same route.

Bildoon found them there, waved the pacing Wreave to a halt. "There's a mob of newspeople outside," he growled. "I don't know where they got the story, but it's a good one. It can be described in a simple sentence: 'Calebans linked to threatened end of universe!' McKie, did you have anything to do with this?"

"Abnethe," McKie said, not looking up from a complicated chalf doodle he was completing.

"That's crazy!"

"I never said she was sane. You know how many news services, 'caster systems, and other media she controls?"

"Well . . . certainly, but . . ."

"Anybody linking *her* to this threat?"

"No, but . . ."

"You don't find that strange?"

"How could any of these people know she . . ."

"How could they *not* know about Abnethe's corner on Calebans?" McKie demanded. "Especially after talking to you!" He got up, hurled his chalf scribe at the floor, started up an aisle between rows of enforcers.

"Wait!" Bildoon snapped. "Where're you going?"

"To tell 'em about Abnethe."

"Are you out of your mind? That's all she needs to tie us up—a slander and libel case!"

"We can demand her appearance as accuser," McKie said. "Should've thought about this earlier. We're not thinking straight. Perfect defense: truth of accusation."

Bildoon caught up with him, and they moved up the aisle in a protective cordon of enforcers. Tuluk brought up the rear.

"McKie," Tuluk called, "you observe an inhibition of thought processes?"

"Wait'll I check your idea with Legal," Bildoon said. "You may have something, but . . ."

"McKie," Tuluk repeated. "do you . . ."

"Save it!" McKie snapped. He stopped, turned to Bildoon. "How much more time you figure we have?"

"Who knows?"

"Five minutes, maybe?" McKie asked.

"Longer than that, surely."

"But you don't know."

I have enforcers at the Caleban's . . . well, they're keeping Abnethe's attacks to a min—"

"You don't want anything left to chance, right?"

"Naturally, not that I'd . ."

"Well, I'm going to tell those newsies out there the . . ."

"McKie, that female has her tentacles into unsuspected areas of government," Bildoon cautioned. "You've no idea the things we found in . . . we've enough data to keep us busy for . . ."

"Some really important powers in with her, eh?"

"There's no doubt of it."

"And that's why it's time we took the wraps off."

"You'll create a panic!"

"We need a panic. A panic will set all sorts of sentients trying to contact her—friends, associates, enemies, lunatics. We'll be flooded with information. And we *must* develop new data!"

"What if these illegitimates"—Bildoon nodded toward the outer door—"refuse to believe you? They've heard you spout some pretty strange tales, McKie. What if they make fun of you?"

McKie hesitated. He'd never before seen such ineffectual maundering in Bildoon, a sentient noted for wit, brilliant insight, analytical adroitness. Was Bildoon one of those Abnethe had bought? Impossible! But the presence of an ego-frozen Pan Spechi in this situation must have set up enormous traumatic shock waves among the species. And Bildoon was due for ego-collapse soon. What really happened in the Pan Spechi psyche as that moment neared when they reverted to the mindless crèche-breeder form? Did it ignite an emotional frenzy of rejection? Did it inhibit thought?

In a voice pitched only for Bildoon's ears, McKie asked, "Are you ready to step down as Chief of Bureau?"

"Of course not!"

"We've known each other a long time," McKie whispered. "I think we understand and respect each other. You wouldn't be in the king seat if I'd challenged you. You know that. Now—one friend to another: Are you functioning as well as you should in this crisis?"

Angry contortions fled across Bildoon's face, were replaced by a thoughtful frown.

McKie waited. When it came, the ego-shift would send Bildoon into shambling collapse. A new personality would step forth from Bildoon's crèche, a sentient knowing everything Bildoon knew, but profoundly different in emotional outlook. Had this present shock precipitated the crisis? McKie hoped not. He was genuinely fond of Bildoon, but personal considerations had to be put aside here.

"What are you trying to do?" Bildoon muttered.

"I'm not trying to expose you to ridicule or speed up any . . . natural process," McKie said. "But our present situation is too urgent. I'll challenge you for the Bureau directorship and throw everything into an uproar, if you don't answer truthfully."

"Am I functioning well?" Bildoon mused. He shook his head. "You know the answer to that as well as I do. But you've a few lapses to explain, as well, McKie."

"Haven't we all?" McKie asked.

"That's it!" Tuluk said, stepping close to them. He glanced from Bildoon to McKie. "Forgive me, but we Wreaves have extremely acute hearing. I listened. But I must comment: The shock waves, or whatever we wish to call them, which accompanied the departure of the Calebans and left behind such death and insanity that we must buffer ourselves with *angeret* and other . . ."

"So our thought processes are mucked up," Bildoon said.

"More than that," Tuluk said. "These vast occurrences have left . . . reverberations. The news media will not laugh at McKie. All sentients grasp at answers to the strange unrest we sense. 'Periodic sentient madness,' it's called, and explanations are being sought every . . ."

"We're wasting time," McKie said.

"What would you have us do?" Bildoon asked.

"Several things," McKie said. "First, I want Steadyon quarantined, no access to the Beautybarbers of any kind, no movement on or off the planet."

"That's madness! What reason could we give?"

"When does BuSab have to give reasons?" McKie asked. "We have a *duty* to slow the processes of government."

"You know what a delicate line we walk, McKie!"

"The second thing," McKie said, unperturbed, "will be to invoke our emergency clause with the Taprisiots, get notification of every call made by every suspected friend or associate of Abnethe's."

"They'll say we're trying to take over," Bildoon breathed. "If this gets out, there'll be rebellion, physical violence. You know how jealously most sentients guard their privacy. Besides, the emergency clause wasn't designed for this; it's an identification and delay procedure within normal . . ."

"If we don't do this, we'll die, and the Taprisiots with us," McKie said. "That should be made clear to them. We need their willing cooperation."

"I don't know if I can convince them," Bildoon protested.

"You'll have to try."

"But what good will these actions do us?"

"Taprisiots and Beautybarbers both operate in some way similar to the Calebans, but without as much . . . power," McKie said. "I'm convinced of that. They're all tapping the same power source."

"Then what happens when we shut down the Beautybarbers?"

"Abnethe won't go very long without them."

"She probably has her own platoons of Beautybarbers!"

"But Steadyon is their touchstone. Quarantine it, and I think Beautybarber activity will stop everywhere."

Bildoon looked at Tuluk.

"Taprisiots understand more than they've indicated about *connectives*," Tuluk said. "I think they will listen to you if you point out that our last remaining Caleban is about to enter ultimate discontinuity. I think they'll realize the significance of this."

152

"Explain the significance to me, if you don't mind. If Taprisiots can use these . . . these . . .. they must know how to avoid the disaster!"

"Has anybody asked them?" McKie asked.

"Beautybarbers . . . Taprisiots . . ." Bildoon muttered. Then, "What else do you have in mind?"

"I'm going back to the Beachball," McKie said.

"We can't protect you as well there."

"I know."

"That room's too small. If the Caleban would come to . . ."

"She won't move. I've asked."

Bildoon sighed, a deeply human emotional gesture. The Pan Spechi had absorbed more than shape when they had decided to copy the human pattern. The differences, though, were profound, and McKie reminded himself of this. Humans could only see dimly into Pan Spechi thoughts. With crèche-reversion imminent for this proud sentient, what was he truly thinking? A crèche mate would come forth presently, a new personality with all the Bildoon crèche's millennial accumulation of data, all the . . .

McKie pursed his lips, inhaled, blew out.

How did Pan Spechi transfer that data from one unit to another? They were always linked, they said, ego holder and crèche mates, dormant and active, slavering flesheater and thinking aesthete. Linked? How?

"Do *you* understand connectives?" McKie asked, staring into Bildoon's faceted eyes.

Bildoon shrugged. "I see the way your thoughts wander," he said.

"Well?"

"Perhaps we Pan Spechi share this power," Bildoon said, "but if so, the sharing is entirely unconscious. I will say no more. You come close to invasion of crèche privacy."

McKie nodded. Crèche privacy was the ultimate defensive citadel of Pan Spechi existence. They would kill to defend it. No logic or reason could prevent the automatic reaction once it was ignited. Bildoon had displayed great friendship in issuing his warning.

"We're desperate," McKie said.

"I agree," Bildoon said, overtones of profound dignity in his voice. "You may proceed as you've indicated."

"Thanks," McKie said.

"It's on your head, McKie," Bildoon added.

"Provided I can keep my head," McKie said. He opened the outer door onto a clamor of newspeople. They were being held back by a harried line of enforcers, and it occurred to McKie, grasping this scene in its first impact, that all those involved in this turmoil were vulnerable from this direction.

Delusions demand reflex reactions (as though they had autonomic roots) where doubts and questioning not only aren't required, but are actively resisted.

—BuSab Manual

Crowds were already forming on the morning-lighted palisades above the Beachball when McKie arrived.

News travels fast, he thought.

Extra squads of enforcers, called in anticipation of this mob scene, held back sentients trying to get to the cliff's edge, barred access to the lava shelf. Aircraft of many kinds were being blocked by a screen of BuSab fliers.

McKie, standing near the Beachball, looked up at the hectic activity. The morning wind carried a fine mist of sea spray against his cheek. He had taken a jumpdoor to Furuneo's headquarters, left instructions there, and used a Bureau flier for the short trip to the lava shelf.

The Beachball's port remained open, he noted. Mixed squads of enforcers milled about in a confused pattern around the Ball, alert to every quarter of their surroundings. Picked enforcers watched through the port where other enforcers shared this uneasy guardianship.

It was quite early in Cordiality's day here, but real-time relationships confused such arbitrary time systems, McKie thought. It was night at Central's headquarters, evening at the Taprisiot council building where Bildoon must still be arguing . . . and only Immutable Space knew what time it was wherever Abnethe had her base of operations.

Later than any of them think, no doubt, McKie told himself.

He shouldered his way through the enforcers, got a boost up through the port, and surveyed the familiar purple gloom inside the Beachball. It was noticeably warmer in here out of the wind and spray, but not as warm as McKie remembered the place.

155

"Has the Caleban been talking?" McKie asked a Laclac, one of the enforcers guarding the interior.

"I don't call it talking, but the answer is not recently."

"Fanny Mae," McKie said.

Silence.

"You still there, Fanny Mae?" McKie asked.

"McKie? You invoke presence, McKie?"

McKie felt he had registered the words on his eyeballs and relayed them to his hearing centers. They definitely were weaker than he remembered.

"How many floggings has she undergone in the past day?" McKie asked the Laclac.

"Local day?" the Laclac asked.

"What difference does it make?"

"I presumed you were asking for accurate data." The Laclac sounded offended.

"I'm trying to find out if she's been under attack recently," McKie said. "She sounds weaker than when I was here before." He stared toward the giant spoon where the Caleban maintained her *unpresence.*

"Attacks have been intermittent and sporadic but not very successful," the Laclac said. "We've collected more whips and Palenki arms, although I understand they're not being successfully transmitted to the lab."

"McKie invokes presence of Caleban self called Fanny Mae?" the Caleban asked.

"I greet you, Fanny Mae," McKie said.

"You possess new connective entanglements, McKie," the Caleban said, "but *the* pattern of you retains recognition. I greet you, McKie."

"Does your contract with Abnethe still lead us all toward ultimate discontinuity?" McKie asked.

"Intensity of nearness," the Caleban said. "My employer wishes speech with you."

"Abnethe? She wants to talk to me?"

"Correct."

"She could've called me anytime," McKie said.

"Abnethe conveys request through self of me," the Caleban said. "She asks relay among anticipated connective.

This connective you perceive under label of 'now.' You hang this, McKie?''

"I hang it," McKie growled. "So let her talk."

"Abnethe requires you send companions from presence."

"Alone?" McKie demanded. "What makes her think I'd do such a thing?" It was getting hotter in the Beachball. He wiped perspiration from his upper lip.

"Abnethe speaks of sentient motive called *curiosity.*"

"I've my own conditions for such a conference," McKie said. "Tell her I won't agree unless I'm assured she'll make no attack on you or on me during our talk."

"I give such assurance."

"*You* give it?"

"Probability in Abnethe assurance appears . . . incomplete. Approximate descriptive. Assurance by self runs intense . . . strong. Direct? Perhaps."

"Why do you give this assurance?"

"Employer Abnethe indicates strong desire for talk. Contract covers such . . . catering? Very close term. Catering."

"You guarantee our safety, is that it?"

"Intense assurance, no more."

"No attack during our talk," McKie insisted.

"Thus propels connective," the Caleban said.

Behind McKie, the Laclac enforcer grunted, said, "Do you understand that gibberish?"

"Take your squad and get out of here," McKie said.

"Ser, my orders . . ."

"Deface your orders! I'm acting under the cartouche of Saboteur Extraordinary with full discretion from the Bureau Chief himself! Get out!"

"Ser," the Laclac said, "during the most recent flogging nine enforcers went mad here despite ingestion of *angeret* and various other chemicals we'd believed would protect us. I cannot be responsible for . . ."

"You'll be responsible for a tide station on the nearest desert planet if you don't obey me at once," McKie said. "I will see you packed off to *boredom* after an official trial by . . ."

"I will not heed your threats, ser," the Laclac said.

"However, I will consult Bildoon himself if you so order."

"Consult, then, and hurry it! There's a Taprisiot outside."

"Very well." The Laclac saluted, crawled out the port. His companions in the Beachball continued their restive watch, with occasional worried glances at McKie.

They were brave sentients, all of them, McKie thought, to continue this duty in the face of unknown peril. Even the Laclac demonstrated extraordinary courage—with his perversity. Only obeying orders though; no doubt of that.

Although it galled him, McKie waited.

An odd thought struck him: If all sentients died, all power stations of their universe would grind to a halt. It gave him a strange feeling, this contemplation of an end to mechanical things and commercial enterprise.

Green, growing things would take over—trees with golden light in their branches. And the dull sounds of nameless metal devices, things of plastic and glass, would grow muffled with no ears to hear them.

Chairdogs would die, unfed. Protein vats would fail, decompose.

He thought of his own flesh decomposing.

The whole fleshly universe decomposing.

It would be over in an instant, the way universe measured time.

A wild pulse lost on some breeze.

Presently the Laclac reappeared in the port, said, "Ser, I am instructed to obey your orders, but to remain outside in visual contact with you, returning to this place at the first sign of trouble."

"If that's the best we can do, that's it," McKie said. "Get moving."

In a minute McKie found himself alone with the Caleban. The sense that every *place* in this room lay behind him persisted. His spine itched. He felt increasingly that he was taking too much of a risk.

But there was the desperation of their position.

"Where's Abnethe?" McKie asked. "I thought she wanted to talk."

A jumpdoor opened abruptly to the left of the Caleban's spoon. Abnethe's head and shoulders appeared in it, all slightly pink-hazed by the slowdown of all energy within that portal. The light was sufficient, though, that McKie could see subtle changes in Abnethe's appearance. He was gratified to note a harried look to her. Wisps of hair escaped her tight coiffure. Bloodshot veins could be detected in her eyes. There were wrinkles in her forehead.

She needed her Beautybarbers.

"Are you ready to give yourself up?" McKie asked.

"That's a stupid question," she said. "You're alone at my command."

"Not quite alone," McKie said, "There are . . ." He broke off at the sly smile which formed on Abnethe's lips.

"You'll note that Fanny Mae has closed the exterior port of her residence," Abnethe said.

McKie shot a glance to his left, saw that the port was closed. Treachery?

"Fanny Mae!" he called. "You assured me . . ."

"No attack," the Caleban said. "Privacy."

McKie imagined the consternation in the enforcers outside right now. But they would never be able to break into the Beachball. He saved his protests, swallowed. The room remained utterly still.

"Privacy, then," he agreed.

"That's better," Abnethe said. "We must reach agreement, McKie. You're becoming somewhat of a nuisance."

"Oh, more than a nuisance, certainly?"

"Perhaps."

"Your Palenki, the one who was going to chop me up—I found him a nuisance, too. Maybe even more than a nuisance. Now that I think about it, I recall that I *suffered.*"

Abnethe shuddered.

"By the way," McKie said, "we know where you are."

"You lie!"

"Not really. You see, you're not where you think you are, Mliss. You think you've gone back in time. You haven't."

"You lie, I say!"

"I have it pretty well figured out," McKie said. "The place where you are was constructed from your *connectives*—your memories, dreams, wishes . . . perhaps even from things you expressly described."

"What nonsense!" She sounded worried.

"You asked for a place that would be safe from the apocalypse," McKie said. "Fanny Mae warned you about ultimate discontinuity, of course. She probably demonstrated some of her powers, showed you various places available to you along the connectives of you and your associates. That's when you got your big idea."

"You're guessing," Abnethe said. Her face was grim.

McKie smiled.

"You could stand a little session with your Beautybarbers," he said. "You're looking a bit seedy, Mliss."

She scowled.

"Are they refusing to work for you?" McKie persisted.

"They'll come around!" she snapped.

"When?"

"When they see they've no alternative!"

"Perhaps."

"We're wasting time, McKie."

"That's true. What was it you wanted to say to me?"

"We must make an agreement, McKie; just the two of us."

"You'll marry me, is that it?"

"That's your price?" She was obviously surprised.

"I'm not sure," McKie said. "What about Cheo?"

"Cheo begins to bore me."

"That's what worries *me*," McKie said. "I ask myself how long it would be until *I* bored you?"

"I realize you're not being sincere," she said, "that you're stalling. I think, however, we can reach agreement."

"What makes you think that?"

"Fanny Mae suggested it," she said.

McKie peered at the shimmering *unpresence* of the Caleban. "Fanny Mae suggested it?" he murmured.

And he thought, *Fanny Mae determines her own brand of reality from what she sees of these mysterious connectives: a special perception tailored to her particular energy consumption.*

Sweat dripped from his forehead. He rocked forward, sensing that he stood on the brink of a revelation.

"Do you still love me, Fanny Mae?" he asked.

Abnethe's eyes went wide with surprise. "Whaaat?"

"Affinity awareness," the Caleban said. "Love equates with this coherence I possess of you, McKie."

"How do you savor my single-track existence?" McKie asked.

"Intense affinity," the Caleban said. "Product of sincerity of attempts at communication. I-self-Caleban love you human-person, McKie."

Abnethe glared at McKie. "I came here to discuss a mutual problem, McKie," she flared. "I did not anticipate standing aside for a gibberish session between you and this stupid Caleban!"

"Self not in stupor," the Caleban said.

"McKie," Abnethe said, voice low, "I came to suggest a proposition of mutual benefit. Join me. I don't care what capacity you choose, the rewards will be more than you could possibly . . ."

"You don't even suspect what's happened to you," McKie said. "That's the strange thing."

"Damn you! I could make an emperor out of you!"

"Don't you realize where Fanny Mae has hidden you?" McKie asked. "Don't you recognize this *safe . . .*"

"Mliss!"

It was an angry voice from somewhere behind Abnethe, but the speaker was not visible to McKie.

"Is that you, Cheo?" McKie called. "Do you know where you are, Cheo? A Pan Spechi must suspect the truth."

A hand came into view, yanked Abnethe aside. The ego-frozen Pan Spechi took her place in the jumpdoor opening.

"You're much too clever, McKie," Cheo said.

"How dare you, Cheo!" Abnethe screamed.

Cheo swirled, swung an arm. There was the sound of flesh hitting flesh, a stifled scream, another blow. Cheo bent away from the opening, came back into view.

"You've been in that place before, haven't you, Cheo?" McKie asked. "Weren't you a mewling, empty-minded female in the crèche at one period of your existence?"

"Much too clever," Cheo snarled.

"You'll have to kill her, you know," McKie said. "If you

161

don't, it'll all be for nothing. She'll digest you. She'll take over your ego. She'll *be* you.''

"I didn't know this happened with humans," Cheo said.

"Oh, it happens," McKie said. "That's her world, isn't it, Cheo?"

"Her world," Cheo agreed, "but you're mistaken about one thing, McKie. I can control Mliss. So it's my world, isn't it? And another thing: I can control you!"

The jumpdoor's vortal tube suddenly grew smaller, darted at McKie.

McKie dodged aside, shouted, "Fanny Mae! You promised!"

"New connectives," the Caleban said.

McKie excuted a sprawling dive across the room as the jumpdoor appeared beside him. It nipped into existence and out like a ravening mouth, narrowly missing McKie with each attack. He twisted, leaped—dodged panting through the Beachball's purple gloom, finally rolled under the giant spoon, peered right and left. He shuddered. He hadn't realized a jumpdoor could be moved around that rapidly.

"Fanny Mae," he rasped, "shut the S'eye, close it down or whatever you do. You promised—no attack!"

No response.

McKie glimpsed an edge of the vortal tube hovering just beyond the spoon bowl.

"McKie!"

It was Cheo's voice.

"They'll call you long distance in a minute, McKie," Cheo called. "When they do, I'll have you."

McKie stilled a fit of trembling.

They *would* call him! Bildoon had probably summoned a Taprisiot already. They'd be worrying about him—the port closed. And he'd be helpless in the grip of the call.

"Fanny Mae!" McKie hissed. "Close that damn S'eye!"

The vortal tube glittered, shifted up and around to come at him from the side. Cursing, McKie rolled into a ball, kicked backward and over onto his knees, leaped to his feet and flung himself across the spoon handle, scrambled back under it.

The searching tube moved away.

There came a low, crackling sound, like thunder to Mc-

Kie. He glanced right, left, back over his head. There was no sign of the deadly opening.

Abruptly, something snapped sharply above the spoon bowl. A shower of green sparks cascaded around McKie where he lay beneath it. He slid to the side, brought up his raygen. A Palenki arm and whip had been thrust through the jumpdoor's opening. It was raised to deliver another blow against the Caleban.

McKie sprayed the raygen's beam across the arm as the whip moved. Arm and whip grazed the far edge of the spoon, brought another shower of sparks.

The jumpdoor's opening winked out of existence.

McKie crouched, the afterimage of the sparks still dancing on his retinas. Now—now he recalled what he'd been trying to remember since watching Tuluk's experiment with the steel!

"S'eye removed."

Fanny Mae's voice fell on McKie's forehead, seemed to seep inward to his speech centers. Hunter of Devils! She sounded weak!

Slowly McKie lifted himself to his feet. The Palenki arm and whip lay on the floor where they had fallen, but he ignored them.

Shower of sparks!

McKie felt strange emotions washing through him, around him. He felt happily angry, satiated with frustrations, words and phrases tumbling through his mind like pinwheels.

That perverted offspring of an indecent unicn!

Shower of sparks! Shower of sparks!

He knew he had to hold that thought and his sanity no matter what the surging waves of emotion from Fanny Mae did to him.

Shower of . . . shower . . .

Was Fanny Mae dying?

"Fanny Mae?"

The Caleban remained silent, but the emotional onslaught eased.

McKie knew there was something he had to remember. It concerned Tuluk. He had to tell Tuluk.

Shower of sparks!

163

He had it then: *The pattern that identifies the maker! A shower of sparks.*

He felt he'd been running for hours, that his nerves were bruised and tangled. His mind was a bowl of jelly. Thoughts quivered through it. His brain was going to melt and run away like a stream of colored liquid. It would spray out of him—shower on . . .

Shower of . . . of . . . SPARKS!

Louder this time, he called, "Fanny Mae?"

A peculiar silence rippled through the Beachball. It was an emotionless silence, something shut off, removed. It made McKie's skin prickle.

"Answer me, Fanny Mae," he said.

"S'eye absents itself," the Caleban said.

McKie felt shame, a deep and possessive sense of guilt. It flowed over him and through him, filled every cell. Dirty, muddy, sinful, shameful . . .

He shook his head. Why should he feel guilt?

Ahhh. Realization came over him. The emotion came from outside him. It was Fanny Mae!

"Fanny Mae," he said, "I understand you could not prevent that attack. I don't blame you. I understand."

"Surprise connectives," the Caleban said. "You overstand."

"I understand."

"Overstand? Term for intensity of knowledge? Realization!"

"Realization, yes."

Calmness returned to McKie, but it was the calmness of something being withdrawn.

Again he reminded himself that he had a vital message for Tuluk. *Shower of sparks.* But first he had to be certain that that mad Pan Spechi wasn't going to return momentarily.

"Fanny Mae," he said, "can you prevent them from using the S'eye?"

"Obstructive, not preventive," the Caleban said.

"You mean you can slow them down?"

"Explain slow."

"Oh, no," McKie moaned. He cast around in his mind for

164

a Caleban way to phrase his question. How would Fanny Mae say it?

"Will there be . . . ." He shook his head. "The next attack, will it be on a short connective or long one?"

"Attack series breaks here," the Caleban said. "You inquire of duration by your time sense. I overstand this. Long line across attack nodes, this equates with more intense duration for your time sense."

"Intense duration," McKie muttered. "Yeah."

Shower of sparks, he reminded himself. *Shower of sparks.*

"You signify employment of S'eye by Cheo," the Caleban said. "Spacing extends at this place. Cheo goes farther down your track. I overstand intensely for McKie. Yes?"

Farther down my track, McKie thought. He gulped as realization hit him. What had Fanny Mae said earlier? "See us to the door! I am S'eye!"

He breathed softly, lest sudden motion dislodge this brutal clarity of understanding.

Overstanding!

He thought of energy requirements. Enormous! *"I am S'eye!"* And *"Self-energy—by being stellar mass!"* To do what they did in this dimension, Calebans required the energy of a stellar mass. *She inhaled the whip!* She'd said it herself: they sought energy here. The Calebans fed in this dimension! In other dimensions, too, no doubt.

McKie considered the refined discrimination Fanny Mae must possess even to attempt communication with him. It would be as though he immersed his mouth in water and tried to talk to a single microorganism there!

I should have understood, he thought, *when Tuluk said something about realizing where he lived.*

"We have to go right back to the beginning," he said.

"Many beginnings exist for each entity," the Caleban said.

McKie sighed.

Sighing, he was seized by a Taprisiot contact. It was Bildoon.

"I'm glad you waited," McKie said, cutting off Bildoon's first anxious inquiries. "Here's what I want you to . . ."

165

"McKie, what's going on there?" Bildoon insisted. "There are dead enforcers all around you, madmen, a riot . . ."

"I seem to be immune," McKie said, "or else Fanny Mae is protecting me some way. Now, listen to me. We don't have much time. Get Tuluk. He has a device for identifying the patterns which originate in the stress of creation. He's to bring that device here—right here to the Beachball. And fast."

Taken in isolated tandem, Government and Justice are mutually exclusive. There must be a third force at work for any society to achieve both government and justice. This is why the Bureau of Sabotage sometimes is called "The Third Force."

—from an Elementary Textbook

In the hushed stillness within the Beachball, McKie leaned against a curved wall, sipped ice water from a thermocup. He kept his eyes active, though, watching Tuluk set up the needed instruments.

"What's to prevent our being attacked while we work?" Tuluk asked. He rolled a glowing loop on a squat stand into position near the Caleban's *unpresence*. "You should've let Bildoon send in some guards."

"Like those ones who were foaming at the mouth outside?"

"There's a fresh crew outside there now!"

Tuluk did something which made the glowing loop double its diameter.

"They'd only get in the way," McKie said. "Besides, Fanny Mae says the spacing isn't right for Abnethe." He sipped ice water. The room had achieved something approaching sauna temperature, but without the humidity.

"Spacing," Tuluk said. "Is that why Abnethe keeps missing you?" He produced a black wand from his instrument case. The wand was about a meter long. He adjusted a knob on the wand's handle, and the glowing loop contracted. The squat stand beneath the glowing loop began to hum—an itch-producing middle C.

"They miss me because I have a loving protector," McKie said. "It isn't every sentient who can say a Caleban loves him."

167

"What is that you're drinking?" Tuluk asked. "Is that one of your mind disrupters?"

"You're very funny," McKie said. "How much longer are you going to be fiddling with that gear?"

"I am not fiddling. Don't you realize this isn't portable equipment? It must be adjusted."

"So adjust."

"The high temperature in here complicates my readings," Tuluk complained. "Why can't we have the port open?"

"For the same reason I didn't let any guards in here. I'll take my chances without having them complicated by a mob of insane sentients getting in my way."

"But must it be this hot?"

"Can't be helped," McKie said. "Fanny Mae and I have been talking, working things out."

"Talking?"

"Hot air," McKie said.

"Ahhh, you make a joke."

"It can happen to anyone," McKie said. "I keep asking myself if what we see as a star is all of a Caleban or just part of one. I opt for part." He drank deeply of the ice water, discovered there was no more ice in it. Tuluk was right. It was damnably hot in here.

"That's a strange theory," Tuluk said. He silenced the humming of his instrument case. In the abrupt stillness something else in the case could be heard ticking. It was not a peaceful sound. It had the feeling of a timing device affixed to a bomb. It counted moments in a deadly race.

McKie felt each counted moment accumulate like a congealing bubble. It expanded . . . expanded—and broke! Each instant was death lashing at him. Tuluk with his strange wand was a magician, but he had reversed the ancient process. He was turning golden instants into deadly lead. His shape was wrong, too. He had no haunches. The tubular Wreave shape annoyed McKie. Wreaves moved too slowly.

The damnable ticking!

The Caleban's Beachball might be the last house in the universe, the last container for sentient life. And it contained no bed where a sentient might die decently.

Wreaves didn't sleep in beds, of course. They took their

rest in slanted supports and were buried upright.

Tuluk had gray skin.

Lead.

If all things ended now, McKie wondered, which of them would be the last to go? Whose breath would be the final one?

McKie breathed the echoes of all his fears. There was too much hanging on each counted instant here.

No more melodies, no more laughter, no more children racing in play. . . .

"There," Tuluk said.

"You ready?" McKie asked.

"I will be ready presently. Why does the Caleban not speak?"

"Because I asked her to save her strength."

"What does she say of your theory?"

"She thinks I have *achieved truth.*"

Tuluk took a small helix from his instrument case, inserted it into a receptacle at the base of the glowing ring.

"Come one, come on," McKie jittered.

"Your urgings will not reduce the necessary time for this task," Tuluk said. "For example, I am hungry. I came without stopping to break my daily fast. This does not press me to speed which might produce errors, nor does it arouse me to complain."

"Aren't you complaining?" McKie asked. "You want some of my water?"

"I had water two days ago," Tuluk said.

"And we wouldn't want to rush you into another drink."

"I do not understand what pattern you hope to identify," Tuluk said. "We have no records of artisans for a proper comparison of . . ."

"This is something God made," McKie said.

"You should not jest about deities," Tuluk said.

"Are you a believer or just playing safe?" McKie asked.

"I was chiding you for an act which might offend some sentients," Tuluk said. "We have a hard enough time bridging the sentient barriers without raising religious issues."

"Well, we've been spying on God—or whatever—for a long time," McKie said. "That's why we're going to get a spectroscopic record of this. How much longer you going to be at this fiddling?"

"Patience, patience," Tuluk muttered. He reactivated the wand, waved it near the glowing ring. Again the instrument began humming, a higher note this time. It grated on McKie's nerves. He felt it in his teeth and along the skin of his shoulders. It itched inside him where he couldn't scratch.

"Damn this heat!" Tuluk said. "Why will you not have the Caleban open a door to the outside?"

"I told you why."

"Well, it doesn't make this task any easier!"

"You know," McKie said, "when you called me and saved my skin from that Palenki chopper—the first time, remember? Right afterward you said you'd been tangled with Fanny Mae, and you said a very odd thing."

"Oh?" Tuluk had extended a small mandible and was making delicate adjustments to a knob on the case below the glowing ring.

"You said something about not knowing that was where you lived. Remember that?"

"I will never forget it." Tuluk bent his tubular body across the glowing ring, stared back through it while passing the wand back and forth in front of the ring's opening.

"Where was that?" McKie asked.

"Where was what?"

"Where you lived!"

"That? There are no words to describe it."

"Try."

Tuluk straightened, glanced at McKie. "It was a bit like being a mote in a vast sea . . . and experiencing the warmth, the friendship of a benign giant."

"That giant—the Caleban?"

"Of course."

"That's what I thought."

"I will not answer for inaccuracies in this device," Tuluk said. "But I don't believe I can adjust it any closer. Given a few days, some shielding—there's an odd radiation pattern from that wall behind you—and projection dampers, I might, I just *might* achieve a fair degree of accuracy. Now? I cannot be responsible."

"And you'll be able to get a spectroscopic record?"

"Oh, yes."

"Then maybe we're in time," McKie said.

"For what?"

"For the right spacing."

"Ahhh, you mean the flogging and the subsequent shower of sparks?"

"That's what I mean."

"You could not . . . flog her yourself, gently?"

"Fanny Mae says that wouldn't work. It has to be done with violence . . . and the intent to *create intensity of anti-love* . . . or it won't work."

"Oh. How odd. You know, McKie, I believe I could use some of your water, after all. It's the heat in here."

Any conversation is a unique jazz performance. Some are more pleasing to the ears, but that is not necessarily a measure of their importance.

—Laclac Commentary

There was a popping sound, a stopper being pulled from a bottle. Air pressure dropped slightly in the Beachball, and McKie experienced the panic notion that Abnethe had somehow opened them onto a vacuum which would rain away their air and kill them. The physicists said this couldn't be done, that the gas flow, impeded by the adjustment barrier within the jumpdoor, would block the opening with its own collision breakdown. McKie suspected they pretended to know about S'eye phenomena.

He missed the jumpdoor's vortal tube at first. Its plane was horizontal and directly above the Caleban's spoon bowl.

A Palenki arm and whip shot through the opening, delivered a lashing blow to the area occupied by the Caleban's *unpresence.* Green sparks showered the air.

Tuluk, bending over his instruments, muttered excitedly.

The Palenki arm drew back, hesitated.

"Again! Again!"

The voice through the jumpdoor was unmistakably that of Cheo.

The Palenki delivered another blow and another.

McKie lifted his raygen, dividing his attention between Tuluk and that punishing whip. Did Tuluk have his readings? No telling how much more of this the Caleban could survive.

Again the whip lashed. Green sparks glimmered and fell.

"Tuluk, do you have enough data?" McKie demanded.

Arm and whip jerked back through the jumpdoor.

A curious silence settled over the room.

"Tuluk?" McKie hissed.

172

"I believe I have it," Tuluk said. "It's a good recording. I will not vouch for comparison and identification, however."

McKie grew aware that the room was not really silent. The thrumming of Tuluk's instruments formed a background for a murmur of voices coming through the jumpdoor.

"Abnethe?" McKie called.

The opening tipped, gave him a three-quarter view of Abnethe's face. There was a purple bruise from her left temple down across her cheek. A silver noose held her throat, its end firmly in the grip of a Pan Spechi hand.

Abnethe, McKie saw, was trying to control a rage which threatened to burst her veins. Her face was alternately pale and flushed. She held her mouth tight, lips in a thin line. Compressed violence radiated from every pore.

She saw McKie. "See what you've done?" she shrieked.

McKie pushed himself away from the wall, fascinated. He approached the jumpdoor. "What *I* did? That looks more like Cheo's handiwork."

"It's all your fault!"

"Oh? That was clever of me."

"I tried to be reasonable," she rasped. "I tried to help you, save you. But no! You treated me like a criminal. This is the thanks I got from you."

She gestured at the noose around her throat.

"WHAT DID I DO TO DESERVE THIS?"

"Cheo!" McKie called. "What'd she do?"

Cheo's voice came from a point beyond the arm gripping the noose. "Tell him, Mliss."

Tuluk, who had been ignoring the exchange, busying himself with his instruments, turned to McKie. "Remarkable," he said. "Truly remarkable."

"Tell him!" Cheo roared as Abnethe held a stubborn silence.

Both Abnethe and Tuluk began talking at once. It came through to McKie as a mixed jumble of noises: "Youinterstellferederhydrowithgenlawnmassfulexecufrom . . ."

"Shut up!" McKie shouted.

Abnethe jerked back, shocked to silence, but Tuluk went right on: ". . . and that makes it quite certain there's no mistaking the spectral absorption pattern. It's a start, all

173

right. Nothing else would give us the same picture."

"But which star?" McKie asked.

"Ahhh, that *is* the question," Tuluk said.

Cheo pushed Abnethe aside, took her place in the jump-door. He glanced at Tuluk, at the instruments. "What's all this, McKie? Another way to interfere with our Palenkis? Or did you come back for a new game of ring-around-your-neck?"

"We've discovered something you might like to know," McKie said.

"What could *you* discover that would possibly interest me?"

"Tell him, Tuluk," McKie said.

"Fanny Mae exists somehow in intimate association with a stellar mass," Tuluk said. "She may even *be* a stellar mass—at least as far as our dimension is concerned."

"Not dimension," the Caleban said. "Wave."

Her voice barely reached McKie's awareness, but the words were accompanied by a rolling wave of misery that rocked him and set Tuluk to shuddering.

"Wha-wha-what w-w-was th-th-that?" Tuluk managed.

"Easy, easy," McKie cautioned. He saw that Cheo had not been touched by that wave of emotion. At least, the Pan Spechi remained impassive.

"We'll have Fanny Mae identified shortly," McKie said.

"Identity," the Caleban said, her communication coming through with more strength but with an icy withdrawal of emotion. "Identity refers to unique self-understanding quality as it deals with self-label, self-abode and self-manifestations. You not me hang yet, McKie. You hang term yet? Self-I overstand your time node."

"Hang?" Cheo asked, jerking the noose around Abnethe's neck.

"A simple old-fashioned idiom," McKie said. "I imagine Mliss gets the hang of it."

"What're you talking about?" Cheo asked.

Tuluk took the question as having been directed to him. "In some way," he said, "Calebans manifest themselves in our universe as stars. Every star has a pulse, a certain unique rhythm, a never-duplicated identity. We have Fanny Mae's pattern recorded now. We're going to run a tracer on that pattern and try to identify her as a star."

"A stupid theory like that is supposed to interest *me*?" Cheo demanded.

"It had better interest you," McKie said. "It's more than a theory now. You think you're sitting in a safe hidey-hole. All you have to do is eliminate Fanny Mae, that's supposed to elminate our universe and leave you out there the only sentients left at all? Is that it? Ohhh, are you ever wrong."

"Calebans don't lie!" Cheo snarled.

"But I think they can make mistakes," McKie said.

"Proliferation of single-tracks," the Caleban said.

McKie shuddered at the icy wave which accompanied the words. "If we discontinue, will Abnethe and her friends still exist?" he asked.

"Different patterns with short limit on extended connectives," the Caleban said.

McKie felt the icy wave invade his stomach. He saw that Tuluk was trembling, facial slit opening and closing.

"That was plain enough, wasn't it?" McKie asked. "You'll change somehow, and you won't live very long after us."

"No branchings," the Caleban said.

"No offspring," McKie translated.

"This is a trick!" Cheo snarled. "She's lying!"

"Calebans don't lie," McKie reminded him.

"But they can make mistakes!"

"The right kind of mistake could ruin everything for you," McKie said.

"I'll take my chances," Cheo said. "And you can take . . ."

The jumpdoor winked out of existence.

"S'eye alignment difficult," the Caleban said. "You hang difficult? More intense energy requirement reference. You hang?"

"I understand," McKie said. "I hang." He mopped his forehead with a sleeve.

Tuluk extended his long mandible, waved it agitatedly. "Cold," he said. "Cold-cold-cold-cold."

"I think she's holding on by a thin thread," McKie said.

Tuluk's torso rippled as he inhaled a deep breath into his outer trio of lungs. "Shall we take our records back to the lab?" he asked.

"A stellar mass," McKie muttered. "Imagine it. And all we see here is this . . . this bit of nothing."

"Not put something here," the Caleban said. "Self-I put something here and uncreate you. McKie discontinues in presence of I-self."

"Do you hang that, Tuluk?" McKie asked.

"Hang? Oh, yes. She seems to be saying that she can't make herself visible to us because that'd kill us."

"That's the way I read it," McKie said. "Let's get back and start that comparison search."

"You expend substance without purpose," the Caleban said.

"What now?" McKie asked.

"Flogging approaches, and I-self discontinue," the Caleban said.

McKie put down a fit of trembling. "How far away, Fanny Mae?"

"Time reference by single-track difficult, McKie. Your term: soon."

"Right away?" McKie asked and he held his breath.

"Ask you of intensity immediate?" the Caleban inquired.

"Probably," McKie whispered.

"Probability," the Caleban said. "Energy necessity of self-I extends alignment. Flogging not . . . immediate."

"Soon, but not right away," Tuluk said.

"She's telling us she can take one more flogging and that's the last one," McKie said. "Let's move. Fanny Mae, is there a jumpdoor available to us?"

"Available, McKie. Go with love."

One more flogging, McKie thought as he helped Tuluk gather up the instruments. But why was a flogging so deadly to the Caleban? Why a flogging, when other energy forms apparently didn't touch them?

The most common use of abstraction is to conceal contradictions. It must be noted that the abstracting process has been demonstrated to be infinite.

—**Culture Lag, an unpublished work by Jorj X. McKie**

At some indeterminate moment, and that soon, the Caleban was going to be lashed by a whip, and it would die. The half-mad possibility was about to become apocalyptic reality, and their sentient universe would end.

McKie stood disconsolately in Tuluk's personal lab, intensely aware of the mob of enforcer guards around them.

"Go with love."

The computer console above Tuluk's position at the bench flickered and chittered.

Even if they identified Fanny Mae's star, what could they do with that new knowledge? McKie asked himself. Cheo was going to win. They couldn't stop him.

"Is it possible," Tuluk asked, "that the Calebans created this universe? Is this their 'garden patch'? I keep remembering Fanny Mae saying it would *uncreate* us to be in her presence."

He leaned against his bench, mandibles withdrawn, face slit open just enough to permit him to speak.

"Why's the damn computer taking so long?" McKie demanded.

"The pulse problem's very complicated, McKie. The comparison required special programming. You haven't answered my question."

"I don't have an answer! I hope those numbies we left in the Beachball know what to do."

"They'll do what you told them to do," Tuluk chided. "You're a strange sentient, McKie. I'm told you've been married more than fifty times. Is it a breach of good manners to discuss this?''

''I never found a woman who could put up with a Saboteur Extraordinary,'' McKie muttered. ''We're hard creatures to love.''

''Yet the Caleban loves you.''

''She doesn't know what we mean by love!'' He shook his head. ''I should've stayed at the Beachball.''

''Our people will interpose their own bodies between the Caleban and any attacks,'' Tuluk said. ''Would you call that love?''

''That's self-preservation,'' McKie snarled.

''It's a Wreave belief that all love is a form of self-preservation,'' Tuluk said. ''Perhaps this is what our Caleban understands.''

''Hah!''

''It's a probability, McKie, that you've never been overly concerned about self-preservation, thus have never really loved.''

''Look! Would you stop trying to distract me with your babbling nonsense?''

''Patience, McKie. Patience.''

''Patience, he says!''

McKie jerked himself into motion, paced the length of the lab, the guardian enforcers dodging out of his way. He returned to Tuluk, stooped. ''What do stars feed on?''

''Stars? Stars don't feed.''

''She inahles something here, and she feeds here,'' McKie muttered. He nodded. ''Hydrogen.''

''What's this?''

''Hydrogen,'' McKie repeated. ''If we opened a big enough jumpdoor. . . . Where's Bildoon?''

''He's conferring with the ConSent representative over our high-handed actions in quarantining the Beautybarbers. It's also a distinct possibility that our dealings with the Taprisiots have leaked out. Governments do not like this sort of action, McKie. Bildoon is trying to save your skin and his own.''

''But there's plenty of hydrogen,'' McKie said.

''What is this of jumpdoors and hydrogen?''

''Feed a cold and starve a fever,'' McKie said.

"You are not making sense, McKie! Did you take your *angeret* and normalizers?"

"I took 'em!"

The computer's readout chamber made a chewing sound, spewed forth a quadruple line of glowing characters which danced in the chamber and resolved themselves into legible arrangements. McKie read the message.

"Thyone," Tuluk said, reading over his shoulder.

"A star in the Pleiades," McKie said.

"We call it Drnlle," Tuluk said. "See the Wreave characters in the third row? Drnlle."

"Any doubt of this identification?"

"You joke."

"Bildoon!" McKie hissed. "We have to try it!"

He spun around, pounded out of the lab, dodged through Tuluk's assistants in the outer area. Tuluk darted in his wake, drawing their enforcer guardians into a thin line close behind.

"McKie!" Tuluk called. "Where are you going?"

"To Bildoon . . . then back to Fanny Mae."

The value of self government at an individual level cannot be overestimated.

—BuSab Manual

Nothing could stop him now, Cheo told himself.

Mliss could die in a few minutes, deprived of air in the Beautybarber tank where he'd confined her. The others on their refuge world would have to follow him, then. He would control the S'eye and the threads of power.

Cheo stood in his quarters with the S'eye controls near at hand. It was night outside, but all things remained relative, he reminded himself. Dawn would be breaking soon where the Caleban's Beachball rested above the surf on Cordiality.

The Caleban's ultimate dawn . . . the dawn of ultimate discontinuity. That dawn would slip into eternal night on all the planets which shared a universe with the doomed Caleban.

In just a few minutes, this planet-of-the-past where he stood would reach its point of proper connectives with Cordiality. And the Palenki waiting across the room there would do what it had been commanded to do.

Cheo rubbed the scars on his forehead.

There'd be no more Pan Spechi then to point accusing fingers at him, to call him with ghostly voices. Never again would there be a threat to the ego which he had secured to himself.

No one could stop him.

Mliss could never come back from death to stop him. She must be gasping in the sealed tank by now, straining for the oxygen which did not exist there.

And that stupid McKie! The Saboteur Extraordinary had proved to be elusive and annoying, but no way remained for him to stop the apocalypse.

Just a few more minutes now.

Cheo looked at the reference dials on the S'eye controls. They moved so slowly it was difficult to detect any change while you kept your eyes on them. But they moved.

He crossed to the open doors onto the balcony, drew a questioning stare from the Palenki, and stepped outside. There was no moon, but many stars shone in patterns alien to a Pan Spechi. Mliss had ordered a strange world here with its bits of ancient history from her Terran past, its odds and ends of esoterica culled from the ages.

Those stars, now. The Caleban had assured them no other planets existed here . . . yet there were stars. If those were stars. Perhaps they were only bits of glowing gas arranged in the patterns Mliss had requested.

It would be a lonely place here after the other universe was gone, Cheo realized. And there would be no escaping those starry patterns, reminders of Mliss.

But it would be safe here. No pursuit, because there would be no pursuers.

He glanced back into the lighted room.

How patiently the Palenki waited, eyes lidded, motionless. The whip dangled limply from its single hand. Crazy anachronism of a weapon! But it worked. Without that wild conjunction of Mliss and her kinky desires, they would never have discovered the thing about the weapon, never have found this world and the way to isolate it forever.

Cheo savored the thought of *forever*. That was a very long time. Too long, perhaps. The thought disturbed him. Loneliness . . . forever.

He cut off these thoughts, looked once more at the S'eye dials. The pointers had moved a hair closer to the curtained moment. They would coincide presently.

Not looking at the pointers, not looking anywhere, really, Cheo waited. Night on the balcony was full of the odors Mliss had gathered—exotic blooms, scents and musks of rare life forms, exhalations of a myriad species she had brought to share her Ark.

Ark. That was an odd name she'd given this place. Perhaps he'd change that . . . later. Crèche? No! That carried painful reminders.

Why were there no other planets? he wondered. Surely the
181

Caleban could have provided other planets. But Mliss had not ordered them created.

Only the thinnest of lines separated the pointers on the S'eye dials.

Cheo went back into the room, called the Palenki.

The squat turtle shape stirred itself to action, came to Cheo's side. The thing looked eager. Palenkis enjoyed violence.

Cheo felt suddenly empty, but there was no turning back. He put his hands to the controls—humanoid hands. They would remind him of Mliss, too. He turned a knob. It felt oddly alien beneath his fingers, but he stifled all uneasiness, all regrets, concentrated on the pointers.

They flowed into each other, and he opened the jumpdoor.

"Now!" he commanded.

If words are your symbols of reality, you live in a dream world.

—Wreave Saying

McKie heard the Pan Spechi's shouted command as the jumpdoor's vortal tube leaped into existence within the Beachball. The opening dominated the room, filled the purple gloom with bright light. The light came from behind two figures revealed by the opening: a Palenki and the Pan Spechi, Cheo.

The vortal tube began swelling to dangerous dimensions within the confined room. Wild energies around its rim hurled enforcer guardians aside. Before they could recover, the Palenki arm thrust into the room, lashed out with its whip.

McKie gasped at the shower of green and golden sparks around the Caleban. Golden! Again the whip struck. More sparks glittered, fell, shimmered into nothingness.

"Hold!" McKie shouted as the enforcers recovered and moved to attack. He wanted no more casualties from a closing jumpdoor. The enforcers hesitated.

Once more the Palenki lashed out with its whip.

Sparks glowed, fell.

"Fanny Mae!" McKie called.

"I reply," the Caleban said. McKie felt the abrupt rise in temperature, but the emotion with the words was calm and soothing . . . and powerful.

The enforcers jittered, their attention darting from McKie to the area where the Palenki arm continued its vicious play with the whip. Each stroke sent a shower of golden sparks into the room.

"Tell me of your substance, Fanny Mae," McKie said.

"My substance grows," the Caleban said. "You bring me energy and goodness. I return love for love and love for hate. You give me strength for this, McKie."

183

"Tell me of discontinuity," McKie said.

"Discontinuity withdraws!" There was definite elation in the Caleban's words. "I do not see node of connectives for discontinuity! My companions shall return in love."

McKie inhaled a deep breath. It was working. But each new flow of Caleban words brought its blast from the furance. That, too, spoke of success. He mopped his forehead.

The whip continued to rise and fall.

"Give up, Cheo!" McKie called. "You've lost!" He peered up through the jumpdoor. "We're feeding her faster than you can rob her of substance."

Cheo barked an order to the Palenki. Arm and whip withdrew.

"Fanny Mae!" the Pan Spechi called.

There was no answer, but McKie sensed a wave of pity.

Does she pity Cheo? McKie wondered.

"I command you to answer me, Caleban!" Cheo roared. "Your control orders you to obey!"

"I obey holder of contract only," the Caleban said. "You share no connectives with holder of contract."

"She ordered you to obey me!"

McKie held his breath, watching, waiting for his moment to act. It must be done with precision. The Caleban had been lucidly clear about that—for once. There could be little doubt of the communication. *"Abnethe gathers lines of her world into herself."* That was what Fanny Mae had said, and the meaning seemed clear. When Fanny Mae summoned Abnethe . . . a sacrifice must be made. Abnethe had to die, and her world would die with her.

"Your contract!" Cheo insisted.

"Contract declines of intensity," the Caleban said. "On this new track you must address me as Thyone. Name of love I receive from McKie: Thyone."

"McKie, what have you done?" Cheo demanded. He poised his fingers over the S'eye controls. "Why doesn't she respond to the whipping?"

"She never really did respond to the whippings," McKie said. "She responded to the violence and hate that went with them. The whip served only as a peculiar kind of focusing instrument. It put all the violence and hate into a single vulnerable . . .''

". . . node,'' the Caleban said. ''Vulnerable node.''

''And that robbed her of energy.'' McKie said. ''She manufactures emotion with her energy, you know. That requires a lot of eating. She's almost pure emotion, pure creation, and that's how the universe goes, Cheo.''

Where was Abnethe? McKie wondered.

Cheo motioned to the Palenki, hesitated as McKie said, ''It's no use, Cheo. We're feeding her faster than you can drain her.''

''Feeding her?'' Cheo bent his scarred head forward to peer at McKie.

''We've opened a giant jumpdoor in space,'' McKie said. ''It's gathering free hydrogen and feeding it directly into Thyone.''

''What is this . . . Thyone?'' Cheo demanded.

''The star that is a Caleban,'' McKie said.

''What are you talking about?''

''Haven't you guessed?'' McKie asked. He gave a subtle hand signal to the enforcers. Abnethe still hadn't shown up. Perhaps Cheo had confined her someplace. That changed things to the contingency plan. They were going to have to try getting a sentient through the jumpdoor.

The enforcers, responding to his signal, began moving closer to the opening. Each held a raygen ready.

''Guessed what?'' Cheo asked.

I have to keep him distracted, McKie thought.

''Calebans manifest themselves in our universe several ways,'' he said. ''They're stars, suns—which may really be feeding orifices. They've created these Beachballs—which are probably intended as much to protect us as they are to house the *speaking* manifestation. Even with the Beachball's damping force, they can't hold back all the radiant energy of their speech. That's why it gets so hot in here.''

McKie glanced at his ring of enforcers. They were moving closer and closer to the jumpdoor. Thank all the gods of space that Cheo had made the opening so large!

''Stars?'' Cheo asked.

''This particular Caleban has been identified,'' McKie

185

said. "She's Thyone in the Pleiades."

"But . . . the S'eye effect . . ."

"Star-eyes," McKie said. "At least, that's how I interpret it. I'm probably only partly right, but Thyone here admits she and her kind suspected the truth during their first attempts at communication."

Cheo moved his head slowly from side to side. "The jumpdoors . . ."

"Star-powered," McKie said. "We've known from the first they required stellar energies to breach space that way. The Taprisiots gave us a clue when they spoke of *embedments* and crossing Caleban *connectives* to . . ."

"You talk nonsense," Cheo growled.

"Undoubtedly," McKie agreed. "But it's a nonsense that moves reality in our universe."

"You think you distract me while your companions prepare to attack," Cheo said. "I will now show you another reality in your universe!" He twisted the jumpdoor controls.

"Thyone!" McKie shouted.

The jumpdoor's opening began moving toward McKie.

"I reply to McKie," the Caleban said.

"Stop Cheo," McKie said. "Confine him."

"Cheo confines himself," the Caleban said. "Cheo discontinues connectives."

The jumpdoor continued moving toward McKie, but he saw that Cheo appeared to be having trouble with the controls. McKie moved aside as the opening passed through the space where he had been.

"Stop him!" McKie called.

"Cheo stops himself," the Caleban said.

McKie sensed a definite wave of compassion with the words.

The jumpdoor opening turned on its axis, advanced once more on McKie. It moved a bit faster this time.

McKie dodged aside, scattering enforcers. Why weren't the damned fools trying to get through the opening? Afraid of being cut up? He steeled himself to dive through the opening on the next pass. Cheo had been conditioned to the thought of fear now. He wouldn't expect attack from someone who feared him. McKie swallowed in a dry throat. He knew what would happen to him. The molasses delay in the vortal tube would give Cheo just enough time. McKie would lose both legs—at the very least. He'd get through with a raygen, though, and Cheo would die. Given any luck, Abnethe could be found—and she'd die, too.

Again the jumpdoor plunged toward McKie.

He leaped, collided with an enforcer who had chosen the same instant to attack. They sprawled on hands and knees as the vortal tube slipped over them.

McKie saw Cheo's gloating face, the hand jerking at the controls. He saw a control arm snap over, heard a distant crackling as the jumpdoor ceased to exist.

Someone screamed.

McKie felt himself considerably surprised to be still on hands and knees in the purple gloom of the Beachball's interior. He held his position, allowed his memory to replay that last glimpse of Cheo. It had been a ghostly vision, a smoky substance visible through the Pan Spechi's body—and the visible substance had been that of the Beachball's interior.

"Discontinuity dissolves contract," the Caleban said.

McKie climbed slowly to his feet. "What's that mean, Thyone?"

"Statement of fact with meaning intensity-truth only for Cheo and companions," the Caleban said. "Self cannot give meaning to McKie for substance of another."

McKie nodded.

"That universe of Abnethe's was her own creation," he murmured. "A figment of her imagination."

"Explain figment," the Caleban said.

Cheo experienced the instant of Abnethe's death as a gradual dissolution of substance around and within him. Walls, floor, S'eye controls, ceiling, world—everything faded into nonbeing. He felt all the haste of his existence swollen into one sterile instant. And he found himself for a transitory moment sharing with the shadows of the nearby Palenki and other more distant islands of movement a place of existence which the mystics of his own species had never contemplated. It was, however, a place which an ancient

Hindu or a Buddhist might have recognized—a place of Maya, illusion, a formless void possessed of no qualities.

The moment passed abruptly, and Cheo ceased to exist. Or it could be said that he discontinued in becoming one with the void-illusion. One cannot, after all, breathe an illusion or a void.